Dedalus Orig

D0581054

THE POLITICAL

Pat Gray was born in Belfast in 1953 and studied politics at Leeds University and Birkbeck College, London

He is the author of various academic works, and two previous novels, *Mr Narrator* (Dedalus 1989) and *The Cat* (Dedalus 1997). He lives in London.

Pat Gray

The Political Map
of the Heart

Dedalus

Eastern Arts
Board **Funded**

Published in the UK by Dedalus Ltd, Langford Lodge, St Judith's Lane, Sawtry, Cambs, PE28 5XE
email: DedalusLimited@compuserve.com

ISBN 1 873982 54 2

Dedalus is distributed in the United States by SCB Distributors,
15608 South New Century Drive, Gardena, California 90248
email: info@scbdistributors.com web site: www.scbdistributors.com

Dedalus is distributed in Australia & New Zealand by Peribo Pty Ltd,
58 Beaumont Road, Mount Kuring-gai, N.S.W. 2080
email: peribo@bigpond.com

Dedalus is distributed in Canada by Marginal Distribution,
Unit 102, 277 George Street North, Peterborough, Ontario, KJ9 3G9
email: marginal@marginalbook.com web site: www.marginal.com

Dedalus is distributed in Italy by Apeiron Editoria & Distribuzione.
Localita Pantano, 00060 Sant'Oreste (Roma)
email: apeironeditori@hotmail.com

First published by Dedalus in 2001
Copyright © Pat Gray 2001

Typeset by RefineCatch Limited, Bungay, Suffolk
Printed in Finland by WS Bookwell

CHAPTER ONE

My father was a curious man with a big, oval face which was nearly always red; in early life because of the weather we had, in later life because of the drink and in-between because he was frequently very angry.

My mother was rather angular and upright; sternly bony, with clear, light blue eyes and a conventional manner of dressing. So conventional that it rather drew attention to her as she walked to work at the family planning clinic in Belfast, where we lived.

"Your mother's doing her bit," my father said vaguely, as he rested from mowing the lawn, with his hat pushed back, polishing his spectacles, the lawnmower abandoned for the moment. The sun burned and the garden was filled with the sweet scent of newly cut grass, mixed with the tang of his pipe smoke, which drifted over into the dense, dark green privet hedge.

When the lawn was finished, with neat lines showing where the mower had been, and the weeds dug out (though more frequently he would leave this to my mother) he fell back into his deckchair and began to read the Irish Times, chuckling loudly to himself, while I busied myself with the hosepipe, flooding the borders of the flowerbeds and cooling my feet in the brown mess this had created.

But then mother came home. Briskly she plucked me out of it, holding me away from herself, so the mud wouldn't go down the front of her summer dress and carried me into the kitchen. There she lowered me into the steel sink and sluiced me down with the floor cloth dipped in water from the cold tap, before stripping me bare of my muddy clothes and wrapping me in a towel and setting me up on a chair outside in the evening sun to warm.

Then the kitchen began to echo with the sound of cooking pots being hauled from cupboards, followed by the angry swish of the broom on the tiled floor. My father ambled in.

"Busy?" he asked.

"It's hectic," my mother replied, pushing her hair back from her face, as she swept the floor, back and forth.

"Everyone's going on holiday and they want to get fixed up." As she said this, she lowered her voice, and glanced through the window to make sure I wasn't in earshot.

Our cleaning lady was called Mrs Cross, which to me at the time, seemed extremely appropriate. She is almost the first person outside the family I can remember, although of course there must have been others who visited. She took her tea break with my mother in the kitchen, the two of them perched there on stools by the counter, eating biscuits or cake.

"That's awful!" My mother's voice was loud. She had an extremely penetrating, and very English voice. I could hear clearly what she was saying even from my attic bedroom. Then Mrs Cross replied in a Belfast accent, full of the broad a's and much harder to hear, and my mother's voice echoed up the stairwell.

"She could come to the clinic! Why doesn't she come to the clinic." I tried to hear, and understand. I hovered at the head of the stairs, pushing on the banisters, the knobbly newel post making marks on my bare pink knees.

"There are ways of doing these things you know. You don't need to go on and on having more and more babies."

Slowly I slithered down the stairs, two steps at a time, leaning forwards with my hands gripping the banister, down past my brothers' bedrooms and my parents' room, down past the bathroom and into the carpeted hall where the grandfather clock ticked slowly in the gloom, then on through the dining room to hang at the kitchen door, swinging it to and fro and trying to insinuate myself into the kitchen, on the pretext of a biscuit.

They both stopped talking, Mrs Cross looking down on me with what seemed like a pitying look, reserved for children who did not have parents that understood the value of a good hard slap or two.

"And what are you after young man?"

"Nothing."

"You are, young man."

"I'm not. I'm not, so."

Later, I faintly detected the churning of the Hoover at the top of the house, punctuated by the sound of large pieces of furniture being moved. I climbed back up to my attic to find Mrs Cross at work, with my train set shunted to one side, destroyed, jumbled and disconnected on the carpet and every item on the shelf by my bedside moved. All dust had gone. It was as if the bedroom was newly minted, and in the process my presence in it all but erased. Mrs Cross seemed to occupy the whole room in her large floral apron and black lace-up shoes, her face like a red cabbage, as she lashed about with the vacuum cleaner hose.

"Why can't she leave it alone," I whined, at supper. My father munched noisily over his chops, reading the newspaper, his head cocked on one side, which I knew meant he was listening carefully to every word I said. It seemed a tremendous thing, that he could simultaneously read a newspaper and engage in conversation.

"She's got to clean, Patrick," said mother.

"Why?" asked my father suddenly. "What ever for?" I knew he was grinning, behind his newspaper. In the early days, he would tease my mother, and make her laugh, even tickle her ribs, under the apron.

"Your mother is a stern woman," he said, half jokingly, as mother cleared the table and went to and fro to the kitchen with the dirty plates, before serving out the pudding, while he peered at the news short-sightedly through his spectacles. Myself and the brothers gobbled down the custard and left the plums my mother had stewed up.

"Ah dear!" He sighed and removed his spectacles, stretching and rubbing his eyes with his knuckles. "Your poor old father!" We paused in our scooping and shovelling, and grinned at each other, knowing what was coming, as he knew we knew. He looked at us, blinking and almost blind without his glasses.

"For God's sake don't end up like your old man," he said. Mother ignored him as we all did, assuming it meant as little as his many other aphorisms; small phrases such as, "Well, that's very true," and, "You would if you could but then you might not," or any of the others that he'd picked up from the bar of the senior common room or anywhere else he might have stopped for a chat or a smoke of his pipe. This was maybe to be our biggest mistake, to underestimate the importance of this one single pronouncement, there mixed in with all the rest casually, as if to hide it.

In the kitchen my mother would lecture at Tom, the brother nearest in age to me. I'd be balanced there on the high stool at her side while she talked to him, slouching there with maybe a patch torn out at the elbow of his jumper, or his knees all cut away and bleeding from climbing trees.

"Tom's not done well this year, Patrick. Have you Tom?" Tom kicked away at the doorpost, but my mother carried on relentlessly. "Your father was down for a first class degree at Oxford, Tom. The most brilliant man of his year. He had a scholarship and then he just threw it all away. Just couldn't be bothered. Just could not be bothered to do it, Tom!" She held me at the back, to make sure I did not fall off the stool. "Now, you don't want to end up like that, do you Tom? You'll need exams. You will end up like . . . " And here she paused. Even then I thought she was about to say, "Like Mrs Cross," but she did not.

"Like the binman," she said.

So though the phrase "wasted genius" did not pass anyone's lips, somehow, through repetition of related concepts, it seemed to seep into the household's understanding. The family watched each other for any sign that one or other of us might be wasting genius. My oldest brother James, already starting his big school, was locked in his room to study, in the hot afternoons. At the age of eleven, he read Virginia Woolf. At the age of five I tried to read Neville Shute. Tom read nothing, and happily kicked footballs up against the garage door, with an incessant, banging sound. Genius was not to be wasted.

It seems obvious to me now, of course, that we were not wasting genius. The weather was fine, the streets outside were peaceful, and the leaves of the big plane trees rustled in the hot air of a seemingly endless summer. In the distance was the great green bulk of Cave Hill.

"It was the first thing I saw, coming off the boat from England after the war," my mother often said. "The mountains, rising over the town. The rest of it was so dark and Victorian."

The city then was not as it later became — a gap-toothed mouth, stopped with shuttered offices and barrack blocks — but a series of deep canyons of red brick, blackened with smoke, dripping on wet Saturdays in winter — or cool and shady in summer — but always solid, and built to last.

My mother held my hand on expeditions into the town.

"Don't dawdle. Pick your feet up and walk properly. You don't want people to think you're a cripple," she said, as we disappeared into Anderson and Macauley, and swept up the wooden escalators, supported on marble columns, to the lingerie department, where my mother bought strange undergarments, and received them back neatly tied with ribbon and bow.

When we visited her bank, I leaned back to look up at the domed ceiling in pastel and gilt, swirling above my head.

"Hullo, Mrs Grant," said the teller behind the counter. "How are we today? And how is the little man?" and his voice echoed up into the dome, merging with the voices of the other clerks and tellers, all murmuring, "Hullo, Mrs McCartney," and, "Why hullo there Mr McConochy, and hasn't it been lovely weather for August?"

At home in Cultra Avenue, from my window, I looked down directly into the trees, so deep, green, and vast, that I could never see where the branches were until the winter came. One day I overheard my father down below, asking about the effect of the tree roots on the house's foundations (at mother's prompting, no doubt). The neighbour paused in his hedge clipping, and said:

"These houses have been here a good few years Mr Grant. And they' ll be with us a good few years yet." And my father would thereafter repeat the neighbour's words approvingly, as a sound justification for postponing this or that repair or refurbishment.

One Sunday just after we moved in, my father took us out behind the garage, and propped me in the wheelbarrow to watch him make a bonfire of the hedge clippings. He poured some paraffin over them, and said:

"Watch this, boys!" (as he always did with anything explosive) and we watched the trimmings going up, burning intensely, with a vicious crackling and spitting that had us ducking for cover. A pall of smoke hung over the garden. Then a deep voice came suddenly out of the hedge, its owner invisible behind his wall of privet.

"Remember!" said the voice. "Remember to keep the Sabbath day holy!" My father seemed struck dumb, as if for a moment he thought the voice had been inside his own head. He opened his mouth to speak, perhaps to ask, "Why?" but the hedge was so deep it was impossible to see who, if anyone, had spoken, or to engage them in debate.

On Sundays our family took to walking by the mansion at Barnet's Park, across the sloping meadow and down to the bottom of the valley, where the canal ran through from Lisburn, shadowing the river past the linen mills. We stared at the high chimneys and the tumbling weirs. We strolled along the towpath, while the river streamed past on one side, and the old canal lay stagnant and clogged with weed on the other. The occasional walker stepped around us politely, or waited for us to pass.

"Grand day!" they said. "Isn't that a cracking day for it now!" In their black Sunday clothes, stepping so the mud wouldn't get on their shoes.

In the early days, my mother would take us to church, and line the brothers up in the crowded pews, in descending order of size, with myself at the end next to her. I can remember the smell of the church, and how full it was, and the mournful note of the hymns. When we came home, my father'd be humming to himself, and pottering with a watering can, wearing a pair of old shorts and a shirt with stains down the front.

I played hopscotch with my brother Tom. At first a few steps, just to the next door drive, then back. In the house next to ours the curtains twitched as we played.

"Look! It's Mrs Crawshaw," Tom whispered, ducking behind the privet so he could peer through at the house without being seen.

"Yes," I said, distracted from our game. I bent down with him, and peered across the garden. A pale, washed-out face looked out at us from a darkened parlour window.

"You stepped on a line," crowed Tom, suddenly jumping up and pushing me aside.

"Didn't."

"Did."

"Didn't."

"Did." Then Tom pushed me over so I fell across a line between the paving stones.

"You's did now," he said, and stood there grinning.

I ran crying back up the drive, along the side path, in through the yard and into the kitchen where mother was cooking.

"Tom!" she called disapprovingly, and together we walked round out onto the drive. I sniffed, and held her hand. But the street was empty, the only sign of life was the pavement still marked out with our abandoned game of hopscotch.

My father was sent for and came out reluctantly, to poke in the hedgerows with a broom handle, as if Tom were some kind of small beast that could be dislodged in such a manner. We peered into Mrs Crawshaw's garden, over the iron gates, painted black. The garden was sombre, and dark, but carefully tended, with a few old-fashioned chrysanthemums to lighten the gloom. Of Tom there was no sign.

"He'll come back," said father, confidently.

Half an hour later, the doorbell rang, and there on the steps stood a grey haired lady, wearing black patent shoes and a tweed skirt and jacket, with a silver brooch at her neck. Her face was sad, and apologetic.

I hung at my mother's skirt.

"Its about the gnomes, Mrs Grant," said Mrs Crawshaw. "The garden gnomes have gone, and I think its your Tom as has got them."

"The gnomes? Oh dear! Look, please come in," said mother, ushering her into the drawing room, while my father scooped up the cards from the table where he had been playing patience, and scuttled for the safety of his study.

"I think your Tom has stolen the gnomes from my front garden," said Mrs Crawshaw.

"Stolen the gnomes! Stolen the gnomes!" said father later, over supper. He beamed. He was extremely pleased. Everyone could see that he was pleased. Tom looked at his feet, grinning. "Went out into the garage and there they were. A whole squad of gnomes all lined up!"

"Whatever got into you, Tom?" asked mother.

"I was making an army," said Tom. "An army of gnomes."

"That's not a reason for stealing now Tom, is it?"

"Certainly not!" said my father. "Garden gnomes are bloody ghastly things anyway." And then it became one of his favourite family stories, like a tale which carried within it the essence of his guide to what the good life actually was, if one could but understand it.

One day father ripped the wheels off the pram, announcing loudly that that was that as far as he was concerned, and took the wheels away with him to the garage, the doors banging shut behind him. He stayed in there for several hours, emerging only for a hurried lunch, to snatch a few lettuce leaves and shove them between two slices of bread with his large, oil-stained fingers before returning to his workbench, pulling the garage doors tightly shut once more, while mother diverted us with small household duties.

It was Tom who led me out to the dank area round the back of the garage, as night began to fall, to the point where the neighbour's hedge closed in tight upon our garden, and hoisted me up so I could see in through the mildewed windowpanes. There inside, my father was making something by the light of a standard lamp. On the workbench stood a small vehicle, made for two, with pram wheels, steered by what seemed to be a pyjama cord. He was bent over the contraption, squinting through his spectacles as he painted a name along its side, in perfect copperplate.

"Hannibal?" said mother doubtfully the next day, as she inspected his handiwork.

"Why have you called it, "Hannibal?""

"Across the mountains!" he cried, as if it were an obvious

13

connection. The script was finely done, along the side of the vehicle, edged in red, white and blue.

"There!" he said. "Now, let's try it out!" He lifted me up, his hands grasping me with gentle firmness, and placed me on the front seat. The wheels wobbled.

"Tom can steer," he said, as Tom was fitted on behind.

Then my father gave us both a tremendous shove, shouting 'WHAMMO!' as he did so, and we set off down the path, through the gate, and out into the road. With a swerve and a bang we mounted the granite kerb back onto the pavement, past Mrs Crawshaw's house, and then away off out under the plane trees and down the hill, the joints between the paving slabs rattling under the wheels. When the road levelled out and we came to a standstill, we both climbed off and dusted ourselves down, and caught our breath.

"Jesus!" said Tom. "That was great!"

The house was hidden by a bend in the road. Tom was excited.

"Come on, Pats!" he shouted. "Push us some more!"

Looking back, I could just see my mother, running down the road towards us. She caught up just as we reached the main road. Her face was flushed, her hair askew. Her hands were still covered in flour from the kitchen. A heavy lorry laboured past on the road, laden with sacks of anthracite, then a country bus. I looked at the traffic; another lorry, with new tractors on it, drove past.

"Come back!" she snapped, gripping each of us by one wrist. "You must not go near that main road!" Tom and I tried to wrench free, just long enough to see the wide road stretched out to the brow of the first hill where the suburbs thinned and the city gave way to country beyond.

That night, my father seemed morose. Now that the work was finished, he sat long at supper, smoking his pipe, and cleaning it out with his big hands, using the dead matches to scour the insides. As we were going upstairs for our baths, he disappeared to the garage to fit a braking mechanism to the new machine, grudgingly, as if it were not what he would normally have done, had he been left to his own devices.

But the brakes never worked. Mother was happy because she could see there were brakes, as such, and therefore that the accident of the first trip would never recur. We used the go-cart mercilessly, Tom and I, while my elder brother James looked on, from his bedroom window upstairs, where he was shut away to study.

A couple of days later me and Tom reached the main road again, while she was at her work, and my father in his deck-chair. This time we hauled the go-cart down to the zebra crossing opposite the sweet shop, and crossed the main road to the other side. Tom winked and reached into his pocket to show me some money he'd wangled from somewhere, and we bought a load of sweeties from a fat old fellow with a white apron who ran the shop.

"You's boys look after yerselves," he said, as he handed them over. Tom and I nodded sensibly.

"Oh, we will Mister," said Tom, while I nodded, not knowing what to say.

"And don't be getting down by the railway," he added.

On the far side of the road, away from where we lived, the houses were small and mean. The front doors opened right onto the living rooms, and the living room windows opened right onto the street. Walking on the pavement, you could lean in on the low sills, and see crowded front parlours stuffed with furniture, and mantelpieces filled with brassware. The side streets were hung with flags; the bunting fluttered, from every lamppost. Children played in the road. A high fence, made of sleepers blocked one end of the street we were in. In the distance, we heard a mournful whistle, drifting on the summer air.

"Train!" shouted Tom, and we ran to the fence. Through a gap I could see the railway line, disappearing to a point in the hazy city beyond, and the rails silver, shimmering in the hot afternoon. The fence smelt of tar.

"There's one coming!" said Tom.

I had never seen a train. I could hear it now, in the distance, labouring up from the city centre. It whistled again, and I saw the plume of white smoke, rising high over the city as it began its run South. Tom had fallen quiet. The street had an expectant air. A couple of boys our age, but with long, dirty trousers and jumpers full of holes, leant in beside us to see the train go by, the pistons working, leaking steam, the exhaust wheezing as the train gathered speed. With another whistle the sky blue engine was past, the carriages following, packed out it seemed with faces at every window, and away up the line with the smoke trailing in the rooftops behind it.

"Slieve Gullion," said Tom, knowledgeably.

"What's that?"

"It's the name of the engine."

"I hope those brakes are working," said mother, doubtfully, as we turned up into the drive. My palms felt sweaty and sticky, and were dirty from the old rope on the go-cart and the tar from the fence and the dust from the trains and the road. I wanted to tell her I'd had an expedition and seen a train. But I couldn't, as Tom's hand was on my shoulder.

The next day we awoke to the sound of music, distant, like the noise of the train the previous day, but incessant, with no coming or going. At times there would be just drums, but not any drums I could recall hearing before. This was a strange kind of thundering and battering, without a tune as such, but nonetheless a sound which set the hairs on the back of my neck tingling. Then there was a pause in which shouts could be heard, and then a high, wild piping reel, and then again the drums and the cries, and the distant moan of the accordion or the bagpipes.

I went down to breakfast, which was a strangely subdued

affair. Even in the dining room, you could hear the drums hammering and banging along the main road by the railway line, at the bottom of our street.

"Why are there bands?"

"It's the twelfth of July," said father, as if that should explain all of it.

On the way down the street we met some of the neighbours, dressed in their summer finery, laughing and gay. Even Mrs Crawshaw was there, with a fine pink hat, almost smiling as the other neighbours called out to her.

"Grand to see you, Mary!"

"That's the perfect day for it now, isn't it?"

"Is this your first twelfth then, wee man?" they asked, bending down, and chucking me under the chin.

"Ah, dear love him isn't he sweet? He'll just adore it, Mrs Grant. Get yourself a ladder, Mr Grant. A ladder the wee fellows can all stand on, and then you can see them, marching by."

So we all walked on down the road together, mother holding my hand, my father absently patting me or Tom on the head and James trailing behind, as if with some secret agenda of his own.

Even halfway down the road we could see the street end was blocked off with deckchairs and old garden seats, with the younger men and some of the smaller boys standing on stepladders as the neighbours had said, and above the heads of the crowd swayed the banners, sailing like great birds over the marchers.

A gang of girls danced along the pavement, singing along with the music.

Then heigh, heigh ho, the lily, lily, O!
The loyal, royal, lily, o!

I felt the music thundering in my chest. My father lifted me up over the crowds. For a moment I could see the marching bands stretched out away and on up the road, forever, as far as the eye could see, either way, the ranks of red-faced men in bowlers, with their shining swords, their sashes and their suits, striding on, as proud as could be. It was a grand sight.

Then one of the marchers broke step, did a quick jump and a skip and was up in amongst us.

"Bernard! Bernard!" he shouted. "Bernard will you's not come and join us?" Behind him the banners waved; silken tales of victory and repentance, of glory in defeat, of temperance and virtue, while the girls sang on, dancing hand in hand.

"I will not," said my father, embarrassed, while my mother looked on.

"Ah well," said the man, disappointed, his face glistening with sweat under the rim of his bowler, before catching sight of us clinging to the lower rungs of a neighbour's stepladder. "And will you look who it is! If it's not young Pat and James and Tom. What a fine bunch of lads!" And he was upon us, pinching our cheeks hard before glancing up he realised his lodge had already begun to march away up towards Dunmurry and he skipped back out through the crowd to rejoin the parade, shouting over: "Good to see you Bernard. You must come round!" Then, as a final afterthought: "And you's too, Mrs Grant, eh . . . Eileen."

"Battle of the Boyne. Bloody rubbish!" muttered father. "He looks a right idiot!"

"Shhh! Bernard, for God's sake, he meant well," said my mother.

There was band upon band of marchers and they continued all day. When the last band reached the field at the end of the march where they were to hear prayers and speeches, the first band was ready to come back, or so my father said. After it was all over Tom made some money from collecting the empty bottles that the crowd had left, and spent the money on sweets, which he ate secretly under the bedclothes in his room. But after that, we rarely stayed in the city when the bands came, though I often asked to do so.

CHAPTER TWO

In the winter it was dark early, by half past three on some days, and the clouds would sometimes be low for weeks on end, with no sign of the hills. We'd have three fires burning, one at each end of the big living room, and one in the dining room, and there'd be a constant clatter of shovels, and my father in and out with the coal scuttle all day.

"How's Moloch," he'd say, peering at the range in the dining room, which roared and hummed and rattled with the draught going up the chimney. He'd open up the fire door, just to take a look, and there'd be a big red eye, staring out, the heart of the fire burning away, heating the water for the bath upstairs. If the eye showed the faintest sign of dimming, perhaps a rim of white ash, or a hint of yellow flame rather than red heat, he'd have the lid off the top and a fresh load of slack chucked in, the flames singeing his knuckles, the hot metal of the lid held at arms length with the poker. "We' ll blow it up," he'd say, opening the draught to 'full'. "For the baths for the boys."

The living room was normally divided by a partition which, as Christmas approached, was hoisted up with a window pole into the cavity wall above, turning the front of the house into one long room with a fire at either end. With this task accomplished, my father's hunt for the perfect Christmas tree would begin.

It seemed no tree on the Lisburn Road was ever quite tall enough or true enough for him. The first time I went with him we visited every shop in walking distance, me wrapped in my thick gabardine coat, and himself in an old army greatcoat. He stood the trees up one by one on the pavement outside the shop, or had the shopkeeper stand them up, and walked round them, judging their aesthetic worth acording to some hidden principle, visible only to himself, while I froze in the wind.

"What do you think?" he asked. The tree was the biggest in the shop, some fir from the Mourne Mountains or the Sperrins, bristling and smelling of pine, glistening with pearls of fresh melted snow, with needles that brought my skin up in a rash as I helped him hold it upright. I looked up through the branches, barely able to see him.

"It's good," I mumbled, not in the least understanding what he was looking for.

"Good!" he said. But then, just as he reached for his wallet, something struck him about the tree. Whether it was the fact that there were only three branches instead of four at the crown, where the angel would sit, or perhaps one of the branches was slightly too short or bent, he hesitated.

"Ah no, " he said. "Ah no, this one won't do at all." And the wallet stayed in his pocket.

But when we finally found a tree, there was no doubting that it was the finest tree on the whole street. It was straight and tall and its branches were evenly spaced, so newly cut that the resin was still leaking from its trunk where it had been felled. Its top brushed the ceiling and it filled the whole of our bay window.

For a day at least my father worked at the decorations in the living room, making fine adjustments with secateurs, pliers and binding wire from the garage, or repairing angels, whose wings had been broken in the summer storage. When it was done, he stood back and lit his pipe, saying:

"There, I think that might just about do."

Closer to Christmas we saw him sneaking upstairs, his arms full of parcels, with his hat still on and streaming with rainwater. We heard the wardrobe door opening in our parents' room and the sounds of hangers clinking and muffled curses.

Later, when he was out and mother was occupied in the

kitchen, James, Tom and I crept in to their room to see what he had been up to. Their bed was wide, covered with a deep red eiderdown. My mother's dressing table was laid with silver-backed combs and brushes, and her perfume lingered in the air. There was a mirror in which you could see yourself, at all angles. Often, after she'd taken me to the barber's, she'd show me:

"There. A lovely short cut," she'd say, turning the side mirror so I could see the back of my own head, shaven.

The dressing table carried framed photographs of many people I'd never met; my mother's English family. They seemed posed, in their suits, with shelves of books in the background, or smiling faintly, in uniform, with medals on their chests, even some of the women, with their hair done up in buns under their army berets.

When Tom opened up the wardrobe it was full of parcels, posted from England or bought in town and not yet wrapped for Christmas. We climbed in amongst the furs, and the high shoes, inside the wardrobe, where it was sweaty and dark. Then Tom found a torch. We rootled about in the furs, reeking of moth balls, peering at the presents to come until Tom discovered a cardboard box and opened it. Inside were old photographs and letters and strange drawings in pen and ink, all of which tumbled out as he slipped off the lid.

"Now look what you've done!" we hissed. But Tom was shining the torch on a drawing of my father in uniform, riding on the back of a tank, looking through his binoculars at a woman not unlike my mother, who was sitting cross-legged upon a map of England with her hair blowing in the wind. James giggled and grabbed the drawing. At the bottom I saw that it was smothered with kisses.

"Let's have a look," he said.

"Gimme!" said Tom, grabbing it back, but just then the door was wrenched open and my father stood there in the light.

21

He pulled us out roughly by the arm, one by one, the letters and drawings falling from the open door onto the floor.

"You wicked boys!" he said. And once he had picked the papers up and carefully checked that everything was there, he closed the lid on the box and took it away to his study, where it remained out of reach for years, gathering dust on top of the tallest bookcase.

"Will you not have the rest of your family over," asked mother, "At least on Christmas afternoon?" My father looked shifty, though in the end he relented, and the aunts and uncles came, in their heavy coats, which hung damply in the down-stairs toilet along with the ladies' hats; extraordinary creations in pink and lilac, blue and maroon, stuck with gilded hatpins.

My father greeted his guests in a bizarrely expressionless way, as he might his accountant, rather than members of his family he'd not seen for a year. He was obviously under strict instructions, because for most of the afternoon he sat in the living room, smiling a wooden smile, and saying, "That's nice" and, "That's very nice," in reply to nearly anything that was said to him.

Later in the afternoon, after the presents had been cleared away, we fought with the cousins and rolled down the backs of sofas, throwing things around. While we played, an uncle and aunt seated themselves on either side of my father at the far end of the long living room, and I heard them ask him did he not think it was time he came back to God? He nodded ambiguously at this, looked at his feet and then his watch, then he stood and said:

"There's that hullabaloo starting again. We'd best separate the boys."

Then they put a stop to our fighting and the visitors assembled in the cold hall, sadly replacing their hats and adjusting them in the mirror. But as they said goodbye till next year they pressed a small volume and a leaflet into my father's hands and looked pityingly at us all, as the door closed behind them.

"Black sheep, eh!" murmured my father proudly to himself, throwing the tract he'd been given into the boiler in the dining room, with an angry clang of its iron lid.

That evening I saw my mother on the phone in the hall, wrapped in her housecoat, as I'd often see her at Christmas and birthdays, talking to her family in England in the darkness. She was shouting down the line:

"Oh good, good, that's good," she was saying, hearing her own family's Christmas described to her. "Yes, we're all fine over here," she said. "We're having another lovely Christmas."

A month or so after Christmas I found mother in the kitchen, with a chicken out on the counter, with its giblets boiling in a pot on the stove, a strange, rich smell in the air and a bag of potatoes up on the drainer. Mrs Cross was peeling away and putting the potatoes in the pot along with some salt. There was an open bottle of wine on the counter and two or three more, still wrapped in brown paper on the sideboard. My father was up a ladder getting into the high cupboard in the dining room.

"What's going on?" I asked. She eased me aside, firmly, as she crossed the kitchen to turn down a boiling pot, her fingers wet on my shoulder.

"There's a dinner tonight," she said, and then pressed me and Tom out into the yard to play. The kitchen windows were steamed up, so we went round to the dining room windows and peered in there instead. My father by now had the table laid out with boxes, which he was unpacking carefully. A silver soup tureen stood in the middle of the table and Mrs Cross set to polishing it.

Eventually the cold outside got to us, so we crept round to the front, let ourselves in and took refuge upstairs. When we came down to ask for dinner it was to find the dining room transformed; the table had had the extra leaf put in and the cloth removed, showing the fine polished mahogany, on which they'd set the wine, the plates from England that my mother'd had at their wedding and the old silver cutlery that was heavy in the hand.

"There, now! Quick!" My mother dashed back and forth (Mrs Cross having by now been sent off). She'd dressed in her finery, showing her bare arms, with her hair up, and wearing pointed silver shoes. My father grappled with a tie which wouldn't knot.

As soon as the doorbell rang, we were shoved out to the hall to line up.

"Bernard. Good to see you!" The house seemed to fill with guests, talking loudly, importantly. My mother's voice rose in pitch. She dashed from kitchen to dining room and back. There were small silver trays, with almonds and raisins and black olives. Tom chewed the olives and spat the pips quietly on the floor, in a dark spot where no one could see. The clock struck seven and the pressure cooker in the kitchen erupted in a gout of steam.

"Come in and take a seat," said my mother. "Sit up straight, Patrick. You've not got curvature of the spine you know. Now, James, tell everyone what you've been reading."

The first course was something I'd never seen before, an avocado, with prawns, and I didn't like it and said so, leaving the prawns on the polished tabletop.

"Pah!" said my father. "Not like avocado! These are the first proper avocados anyone's had for years."

And then they were off. Would the generation after the war be different from the one before? Some of them thought that yes, it would, what with the advent of welfare, and how similar everyone was becoming since they all had a chance in life, and the old social distinctions were on the slide. And still others thought that those distinctions didn't matter so much as religions, and then my mother said:

"Really! How interesting! Religions? What ever do you mean?" and then everyone looked at her a bit oddly before trying to explain, and after that she went out to the kitchen, and then they said well surely religious differences weren't what they were, at which there was a bit of a commotion, and some of the fellows were almost up out of their seats saying well they'd be sad if religious differences got any less, and still others saying differences were alright, but there had to be respect and understanding for the correct ideas, until my mother came back in with the chicken, and everything subsided and they said how fabulous it looked, and was it free range? I was playing trains with the prawns by then, and they'd sent Tom out for flicking peas, but James was there, quite on his toes, listening in, as if he understood all of it.

My mother was a great cook. She was always at it, in the kitchen, looking out at the garden through the steamed up window, working away at something in a bowl, or on the chopping board, while other items bubbled away on the stove, or toasted gently in the oven. There was not a bought packet of biscuits in the house until I was ten, though there'd always be a couple of tins with chocolate flakies, or flapjacks or fruit-cake, all home made, in the wooden cupboards just under the counter where she worked, and these'd be doled out as a reward for effort, or abstinence.

"Not until you've cleaned your shoes."

"Not until you've tidied your room."

"Not till you've not bitten your nails for a week."

Then there'd be half a flapjack, or a slice of fruitcake and a glass of milk. Except for father, who'd never eat biscuits at all, but had strange tastes in items such as gherkins, kippers, Cracker Barrel cheese, and William Younger's beer, which were curiously only ever in the house when mother was away visiting in England.

CHAPTER THREE

My school was up a long gravel drive lined with yews and built to last. It smelt of polish and gym shoes, food and sweat, chalk and paper. When my father and mother had taken me there first to visit, the headmaster had given us tea and cake in his study, and my father had later signed a cheque, with an audible sigh. When the heavy black doors swung shut behind us on the way out he said:

"Thank God that's over."

There wasn't a lot of fun at school, what with the session of prayers in the morning and the constant sums and English. But painting was different. After instructing that the desks were to be cleared of rulers and protractors and every other sign of serious work, they'd give you a big sheet of sugar paper: blue, or grey, or green. Each boy would have a jam jar of water on the desktop, a thick paintbrush and his tray of paints.

The first time it happened I couldn't think what to paint at first, until an idea struck me and I reached for the red paint, but it was too bright red for what I had in mind. I mixed in a bit of black and it seemed to give the right colour. So I drew out a long rectangle and then into that I marked out windows and doors. And then another rectangle. I cleaned my brush like I'd been told and filled it with blue paint for the sky, and painted that all over the top of the page. The classroom seemed to have diminished, its sounds altered, seeming further away. I loaded my paintbrush with black paint and painted three circles, a chimney, a column of black smoke, going up into the sky, and then some more black clouds, like the sky really was. I cleaned my brush again, but the black and the red had turned the water muddy, so when I did the green for the hills over the city they came out dirty, particularly after I'd added the black bits for the cliffs of Cave Hill and for the smoke from the steam engine.

The teacher put down his "News Letter" around halfway through and took a stroll around to see how the boys were doing, looking at his watch and glad that the afternoon had worn away so pleasantly.

"What's that McCann?"

"That's me mammy, Sir."

"McCartney, sure cows have udders under them, don't they."

"Its not a cow, Sir."

"Well what is it, then?"

"It's two fellers sheltering from the rain under a coat, Sir."

"Oh, aye. Hah! I can see that now right enough." And then the teacher stood behind me, and I could feel his presence there, looking over my shoulder.

"That's a fine painting Grant," he said, thoughtfully. "But there's no people in it."

"People, Sir?"

"Aye, Grant, sure in a city this size there's lots of people."

And then he was off back up to his desk at the front.

I rocked back on my stool and had a wee glance at all the other paintings I could see from where I sat. I could see the lad beside me had done a big fellow in Linfield colours, except that his face was more than normally red and the red had run so it looked like his chin had melted and flooded down his shirt front. Then I looked back at my own painting. There was a big gap at the bottom where I could fit in another terrace of houses and belching chimney pots, so I did that, and then I had another idea. I blacked out a stretch at the bottom to make a road and waited for it to dry. I could sense that time was running out. When at last the road was dry I reached for the yellow and whacked in a faint hint of red and got myself up a brilliant orange. Then I did some big round drums in grey and a load of wee stick men, with their arms rigid, marching in lines like large ants across the bottom of the picture and up into all the available space between the houses, with their Orange banners. I was vaguely aware of everyone packing up all around and then the teacher came up again.

"Ah!' he said. "Ah well now class, look at this. Grant has done something very special!" He took my picture carefully off the desk and held it up for all the class to see. Later he put it in pride of place on the board for when the parents were to come round. Underneath he had me copy out:

"Belfast. 12th July. By Patrick Grant. Age 6."

In the summer, the cricket was on in school. They made you do it on fine hot days when the crows were cawing in the treetops and the grass was soft beneath your feet, and just after lunch when you'd had two helpings of spotted dick and custard, and wanted to sleep.

I met my new friend at cricket. His name was Peter. I'd very nearly lost another match, and all the fellows were shouting at me and telling me what a prick I was from the bench (and I could feel those that were polite enough not to shout thinking much the same), when they put Peter on. He wasn't sporty at all, like the others. You'd never see him catching and jumping. He was really solid and slow, and normally was nearly as bad as me at everything with balls. But this time, seeing the predicament I'd left us in he stood up, picked up his bat and walked to the crease, and walloped the ball in every direction; over the fence into the road beyond, out over the orchard wall and into the concrete quadrangle by the drinking fountain. And then, when he was finally bowled out, he walked back to the bench with the same slow, heavy footsteps, without smiling, to the cheers of everyone.

"That was great," I said.

"Oh aye," he said. He had a big, open, friendly face. After that, I don't know if it was gratitude or what, but we tended to play together, up in the woods behind the school, though the head teacher had said he'd beat us to within an inch of our lives if we went within a mile of them, and we always believed him, as you do. We'd seen him grab boys by the hair, and kick their backsides. We'd even seen him grab a boy by the ear in front of the whole school, and pull him over to the changing room door, reach in for a gym shoe with his free hand, and beat the boy about the head and the legs with the flat of the sole, all just for saying, "Fuck."

So when Peter and I came up to the high fence into the old woods one day, we walked up and down the street a few times to check there was no one watching us, pretending we were looking for a house number, or something we'd dropped on the pavement. The problem was we didn't know where the head teacher lived, and he could have been living in one of the houses that overlooked the gate into the old wood. At that very moment, he could have been crouching behind any of the many pairs of net curtains in the street, with a gym shoe in his hand, ready to run out and beat us up there on the pavement. I knew what it'd be like. Once he'd given me a light, playful cuff over the back of the head for blotching my copybook. It was only a small blotch, but my head sang and whistled for ten minutes afterwards.

"Come on! I'll give you a leg up," I said, hoisting Peter up. But he was a big lad, and only just made it to the barbed wire at the top of the gate, where he wobbled for a moment with his trousers caught, then stumbled, and that pulled him clear, though I could hear his trousers ripping as he fell down the other side into the long grass. Then he was whispering to me, through a gap in the fence. I could see half his face, with his lips moving.

"Get your foot in here," he said, the tips of his fingers showing a small toehold and I was up and over and down the other side into the grass along with him, the two of us panting, and expecting immediate retribution from God knows where.

We crossed through the long grass to where a tangle of brambles and honeysuckle clung to the rim of the wood and pushed through into the gloom beyond, then followed a winding path past an old pond which was clogged with frog-spawn and weed. The trees around had been specially planted, it seemed; their exotic branches trailing in the waters of the lake, wild and unkempt. In the distance, we could hear the traffic on the Malone Road, like in another universe.

"Ah, Jasus," said Peter, holding his trousers where the barbed wire had torn the seat out of them. "My ma 'll beat me half to death," he added, bending to inspect the strip of material that'd come out of the bottom of his pants.

We kept on up the path, coming in the end to an old house with high windows and a tall, pitched roof, one half fallen in and the other still inhabited, a faint trail of wood smoke coming from one chimney. Swiftly, we crept closer to the house, until we could almost see in through its dark, uncurtained windows.

"King Billy's house," whispered Peter, crouching low behind some ferns. "They sez he stopped here, on the first night. On his way to the Boyne."

We both stood up, maybe in awe, which was the worst thing we could have done, because at that moment the door of the house flew open, and this old fellow on crutches stood there, staring at us. Then he let out a really ghastly kind of a shout, like you'd imagine in your worst nightmare, a beastly, twisted sort of a shout, like he couldn't speak properly, yet would make a noise just the same, to show you how he felt and what he'd do to you if he wasn't on crutches.

We ran like mad, away out of it, back along the path, past the pond, with the horrible cry following us, through the trees, over the fence and back into the road and all the way back home until we were both in my attic room in Cultra Avenue, with the smell of baking flapjacks and the sound of my father listening to his music on the radio.

★

When Peter had gone, I turned to my trains. The house inside was strangely cool, and the sweat felt cold against my skin. I tried to play. By now I had a train that ran along each wall of my bedroom, complete with houses, people, cars and stations. The locomotives churned around the track. The window was open, and the breeze blew in. I coupled and uncoupled a goods train, moved some trucks from one side of the board to another. I tried two locomotives together, to pull a particularly long train. The locomotives struggled, their wheels slipping, unable to gain purchase. I switched the toy train off, and hung at the head of the stairs, able now to hear the ticking of the clock in the hall far below. I could hear the joists and floorboards creaking, and the distant sounds of lawns being mown. Somewhere a dog barked. I could hear the sound of father drilling away in the garage, and the faint, distant thunder of the drums starting up. Between my teeth, curiously, I found the notes of the marching tune:

> *Sure it was worn, but very beautiful,*
> *And its colours they were fine,*
> *And its on the twelfth day of July,*
> *That I' ll wear the sash my father wore . . .*
> *At Eniskillen and the Boyne.*

Where had it come from? It must have been everywhere, in the atmosphere.

"What's that, Patsy?" It was my eldest brother James, standing on the stairs in front of me. He was fourteen now. "A critical year," mother said. He had a kind, but rather pale face. Unlike Tom, he would never hit me, indeed until the disagreements over politics, he had never said an unpleasant word to anyone.

"S'just a song," I said.

"Yep, " he said. I peered around him, into his room. The curtains were closed. Sheets of paper were piled across the floor, in no particular order, covered in strong, grown-up handwriting, as if he knew exactly what needed to be said. In his room there was more writing than I had ever seen before anywhere. I thought of another family story that my father liked to tell:

"James didn't say anything until he was three, and then he recited a complete Times editorial without hesitation." I had no idea what a Times editorial was. One day though I was sure that I too would recite a complete Times editorial without hesitation, and win a story about myself. But now James seemed to shrug at me, as if to say, "Come in if you want."

The thing I remember about him on that day was the strange absence of toys, and how much older he seemed than me. I stepped into the room.

"You shouldn't be singing that song," he said. It was not particularly a threat. It was a sort of statement.

"Why?" I asked.

"It's an Orange song."

"I see," I said, not seeing.

"Sung by Orangemen."

I stepped into the shadows of his room. There were so many things there which were not child's things. There was a map of Ireland pinned to the wall, which was quite different to the one we had at school, which showed the North, and Britain and a kind of a blank for everything in the South. The map on James's wall reached far down into the blank, showing towns and a whole country of people. This map had England as a blank. Books were open on the cluttered tabletop, with markers in them, where James had left off reading.

"The Orangemen are the baddies, Patsy," he said.

"Yes," I said. Then I spotted a piece of railway line, covered in dust, sticking out from under his bed. Quickly, I stooped down and picked it up, backing awkwardly from his room and pleased to be away.

Then one day I was bounding down from the attic in great leaps, aspiring to cover an entire flight without touching either step or banister, when I caught a glimpse of my mother through the open door of her bedroom, trying on a blue dress. The dress was covered in thousands of tiny sparkles, and she was turning this way and that in front of the mirror. She had an odd way of pulling faces at herself in the mirror when she did this, as if trying to turn herself into someone else. I lingered at the door, surprised too to see other boxes laid out on the bed, containing new white blouses and other things she'd bought. Then she caught sight of me and chased me off, as if I'd seen something she wished to hide.

"Why's Ma getting all dolled up?" I asked Tom. "I hope its not another of them dinners coming up, eh?"

But Tom just tapped the side of his nose mysteriously, and said:

"You'll see soon enough, Pats," and that was that for a while.

The next thing was she took to telephoning.

"When does it leave?" I heard her ask now. "Oh yes, and the arrival time you've given me . . . is that in English or in Irish time? Would Fishguard be better? I know it's very busy around the twelfth."

Out in the yard I found father trying to coax the family cat into a picnic hamper. This was a ridiculous and comic sight, there being no love lost between the cat and my father, himself referring to it as 'that superfluous beast,' or 'the creature.' He'd chased it round the yard a couple of times and now had it almost cornered, both of them glowering at each other, with the basket held open and a dish of food inside as bait.

"What're you doing?" I asked.

"The cat's coming with us to England," he said.

"Are we goin' to England?"

"We are," he said, slamming the basket against the wall, pinning half the cat against it, then shoving the rest of the cat's

33

rear end inside and putting the lid down. The cat meowed piteously.

"When? For how long? Are we all going?"

"We're going for a week," said father, and he tried to get the cat's paws back in the basket where they'd got out under the lid, scrabbling and catching in the wickerwork.

"Could we not just leave him behind with a pile of grub in the yard?" I asked.

"Aye, put him in a home or something," said Tom, who'd been attracted by the commotion. "A cat hotel."

"If we left him there's no telling what would happen. He might get chucked on an Orange bonfire," said father. I tried to get the cat back in the basket too after that, as I'd seen the bonfires they were getting ready down over the main road, against the gable ends of the Fenian houses. They'd be twenty feet high, with all kinds of quite reasonable furniture and stuff stacked up there, none of your rubbish, as if having a good bonfire on twelfth night was more important than having a wardrobe in your bedroom to hang your clothes.

"So you're off over the water?" asked Peter, suspicious as to why anyone should not be in Ulster for the twelfth.

"Yes," I said. "Oxford. England." It gave me a sense of great importance, like I'd been marked out as different in some way.

We travelled together on the Liverpool boat, myself and Tom sharing a high bunk with hard, crisp sheets, stiff with starch. We kicked each other under the blankets till we fell asleep to be wakened with dry biscuits and tea in the morning as the ship edged up the Mersey past the lines of freighters waiting for the tide. We took a taxi, weaving through the unfamiliar Liverpool streets to the station, and then a train to Oxford.

My grandparents' house was a tall stone building off the high street, with endless stairs, and an attic where we played for hours. At meals we shared with the grandparents, my father behaved deferentially, almost awkwardly, even knocking over his chair as he stood to greet his father-in-law on our first day. At breakfast he arrived clean-shaven, with his cheeks glowing, as if my mother had given him a good scrubbing before starting the new day.

We saw some of the people who'd sent us Christmas presents; the people whose photos stood on my mother's dressing table. At supper they talked constantly in loud English voices, about still other people we had never met or seen, and places that seemed impossibly remote: the Lake District, London, Edinburgh, Paris, Rome. And when they asked my father about his work at the University he talked loudly too, gulping at the wine.

And from time to time they'd ask, almost apologetically, whether we were all alright.

"Alright!" cried my father. "Its a grand country to bring up children. You' ve the fields and the mountains as far as the eye can see. There's none of the traffic you have got over here. There's glorious countryside and the schools are great, just great!"

I could see my mother waiting to get a word in, then didn't James start up with some story about a fellow who'd been caught with gelignite, and everyone went:

"Oh no!" And mother was drawn into denying there was anything wrong at all, until the old granddad said he was sure everything was fine, and hadn't the situation been well under control since partition, and would anyone be wanting more roast potatoes?

On the way back I played in the corridors of the trains as we trundled home along the Welsh border, the windows wet with rain, back to Lime Street and the black streets of Liverpool, the tea-brown Mersey and the boat back to Ireland. All night the cat, released from its basket, looked at the waves in the moonlight as we went home. My mother didn't sleep. At four she asked the steward for tea. In the half-light, I saw her at the porthole, looking out.

CHAPTER FOUR

Things were not always scary. In the early days me and Peter would build planes from sixpenny kits, trying to make them bigger and better each time. We'd take them down to the clay hills in the Lagan valley, and throw them off the top, down into the bog below. This was a good place, as there was no reason for you not to be there. It was always busy with people walking their dogs, or with snoggers and boys who'd try and ride their bikes down the hills, and with anyone with any old stuff to chuck that was too big for the Corporation to take away.

We'd stand high on top of the clay hills, where the new estates stopped dead at the edge of the country, and look out at the silver river, snaking in a big curve towards the city centre. If you were lucky and it was a calm evening with no wind, sometimes the planes would just lift into the mild air and drift slowly off away from you, barely descending at all, out over the bog and away towards the river on the other side, the one plane following the other, almost colliding in the air, up with the birds. Afterwards, we had to wade through the bogs to find them, but I'd carry Peter on my back, to save his socks, and run like mad over the boggy bits, in the hope we wouldn't sink too fast before getting to the other side.

Then one day, standing in her spotless kitchen with the dishcloth in her hand, Peter's mother asked me whether I'd like a weekend in the country. I nodded and she said could I ask my mother to give her a ring?

There were a few phone calls to sort matters out, and then it was agreed.

"You'll meet my cousin Elaine," said Peter. "She's a character."

When finally the day came, and I stood with Peter on the

platform at Great Victoria Street, under the high roof, with the doors slamming on the train and the hiss of the steam everywhere, Peter's mother said to him:

"Now watch out for Elaine, and don't you go giving your grandparents any trouble."

My mother pecked me on the cheek and they saw us into safe seats with some women with shopping in the compartment and a few solid chaps in coats with their papers, who all said they'd put us off at the right place.

We leant from the window and waved as the train set out, and I watched my mother and Peter's mother disappear back down the platform, exchanging some worried thought with each other as the engine took us out under the bridge and away. The train was bound for Dublin and full of shoppers. The smell of their damp coats and their humour and the general air of out-for-a-day-of-it made us jolly as we rattled along, with the white smoke hanging in the hedgerows and the dry-stone walls, the bullocks in the fields scattering from the whistling locomotive.

When we got out there was a car waiting and Peter's grandparents, pleased to see us together and all in one piece. A high wall ran around the estate where they lived, though the coping stones had fallen in many places, and the creepers grew in the gaps. We turned up the drive, past the ruins of a gatehouse, with the brickwork dark with the stains of damp. The old man tutted at the ruts in the long drive, where the gravel had been washed away.

"Would you look at the state of it," he said. "The place is gone to the dogs."

When we turned off the track, it was into the square courtyard of an old house built of grey stone, the yard cobbled for the horses that had once pulled in there. Inside, there was a warm kitchen with a big stove, and some cats, which the grandmother snapped at, then stroked, before taking us up to the rooms above, where the floorboards wobbled under the fraying carpets. We unpacked our things into a massive mahogany chest of drawers and bounced on the beds. Later we played innocent games across the yard and up into a ruined orchard, where the trees had grown gnarled and fruitless. The orchard wall was overrun with roses with trunks as thick as a man's leg.

Coming out of the orchard we met Elaine riding a horse, with her sister following behind. She had blonde hair and was lightly built, with her hair tied back tightly with a hairband. She was a year or two older than me and wore jeans and a pair of old riding boots, with a check shirt on top. The horse was very large, and snorted and pulled away when she tried to stop it.

"Wisht!" she said, pulling back hard on the reins and patting the side of its head. "Y'auld bastard!"

"S'Elaine," said Peter, introducing us. "S'Pat." She looked down at me from the saddle.

"Yeah," she said.

"Are you's coming down after tea?" asked Peter. There was a pause, as if the two of them were thinking.

"We'll see," said Elaine. And then she thwacked the horse on its behind and it cantered off fast up the path, throwing up clods of earth, and I could hear her laughing.

"They've a new house, up in the town," said Peter.

"Where's the old one?"

"Here," he said, waving his arm at the orchard.

It was then that I saw one whole wall of the orchard was the wall of a house, but a house so big that it must in its day have been a palace. Under the creepers and the rambling roses and half hidden, half demolished, were the ruins.

"Let's see," I said. But he didn't seem keen. Later, when we got behind the wall, there was a mess of old blocks of sandstone, cornices, fallen brickwork, covered in moss, dank, cold and hard to walk amongst, smelling of old plaster and earth, like a disused graveyard.

"They couldn't keep it up," said Peter. "No-one could."

"Why not?"

"It'd over a hundred rooms," he said.

In the evening one of the workers of the estate came in, with a tin pail with some eggs in the bottom, and Peter's grandmother talked to him in the back scullery, giving him instructions for the hens for the next day. We had omelettes for supper and leant out on the window-ledge before bed, flying paper aeroplanes in the dusk, down into the cobbled courtyard.

At nine, Peter looked at his watch and said disconsolately:

"Well, she's not coming now." I looked up the deserted path that led away from the house, through a copse of silver birch, past the ruins and down to Markethill on the other side. Somewhere, the sound of sheep could be heard, baa-ing mournfully.

When I got home from Markethill, it was to find father deep in holiday preparations, emptying the loft of a number of large khaki bags, which were later revealed to be tents. These he set up on the lawn, amongst the rose beds, and worked upon them with the same feverish determination that had been applied to the building of the go-cart.

"This will do as a lavatory!" he explained to mother, loud enough for all the neighbours to hear, driving the pegs into the lawn with a wooden mallet as he tried to erect a pup tent on its end, to hide the chemical toilet.

I watched him from my bedroom window, where I had retreated after another attack from Tom who had poked me with the sharp end of a piece of toy railway track.

"You can do sums now." He had mimicked my mother praising me.

Leaning from my bedroom window, I wished that I could not get good marks. If I could fail, then I too could spend my afternoons, like my father on the lawn, working out how to disguise a chemical toilet behind a pup tent, pitched on its end. I could see him quite clearly, standing back with his hands on his hips, curiously foreshortened, smoking his pipe. The tent leaned over at an angle. His hand was wrapped in a handkerchief that mother had given him, where he had hit his thumb, or what was left of it. That day was the first time I noticed he had only half a thumb on one hand. Later, at supper, I noticed the slight dent below the cheekbone, on the edge of the collar, where the shrapnel had broken his neck.

"They used to come and look at me in the hospital," he said. "As if I was a miracle."

Then he bought a car.

"Here it is! Look at that!" he said, stabbing at the newspaper with his forefinger, deep to the lower end of the items for sale section of the small ads.

"Ex War Department desert recovery jeep, fully converted for family usage. New brake wires. Good clutch. Four horsepower. Twenty-five pounds or nearest sensible offer."

We continued eating.

"I drove them in the desert," he explained. "They never went wrong. Absolutely safe as anything. Good God, wonder how one got over here? That's extraordinary."

"New brake wires?" repeated mother.

"Perfectly safe! Tighten them up regularly, especially when it's hot, and everything will be fine."

The car arrived the next day. It was very long, with a sort of half-timbered appearance, like a Morris Traveller, but with more wood to it. My father jumped down off the running board smiling broadly, as the neighbours gathered, some politely, at a distance, peering over hedges, others not so polite, kicking the tyres, or rocking the car to test the springs before agreeing jealously, or reluctantly that perhaps a bargain had been found.

The windows operated like old-fashioned train windows, and were secured by means of a leather belt. Indeed, they probably were train windows which had been picked up cheap, and fitted in as the bodywork had been built. There were four rows of seats, so those sitting in the back could fight and pass remarks without being observed or overheard by those at the front. The windscreen rose vertically like that of a Model 'T' Ford, and it had a top speed of around twenty-five miles per hour. This meant that when our holiday preparations were finally complete, the actual journey South took three days and involved many stops along the way.

CHAPTER FIVE

"Damn," came my father's voice from the driver's seat. "Oh Damn!" Looking forwards past the piled bundles of camping equipment: the pots, the broom handles which were to serve as tent poles, the hanks of rope and the boxes of tinned food, we could see him wrestling with something down by his feet. Outside, the main street of Listowel was jammed with cattle, their brown hides rubbing against the side of the car as they passed, making it rock. A green bus had halted at the cross-roads ahead, and a lorry load of sheep was backed up behind that. My father waved something in his hand, some long, steel lever.

"The bloody gear stick's come off!" he shouted.

"Can't you put it back in?" said mother. "Look, jam it in that hole!"

My father tried to do as she suggested. The cattle hooted and snorted. The Gardai arrived and my father let his window down on its leather leash.

"The bloody gear lever's come off," he explained.

"Dear me, sir, that's a spot of bad luck now," said the garda.

"What sort of a vehicle is it now, exactly, sir?"

"It's a Ford," said my father. "A Ford desert recovery jeep."

"Is it indeed!" said the garda at the window, thoughtfully. "Well, now I think I might know just the man to fix that. But first we've to get you's shifted out of the road."

And then he was away through the crowd and ordering the sheep lorry to back up to our bumper and my father was out there in the road too, shouting instructions.

"Don't tie it there. There! On the subframe. You'll pull the whole front off it that way!"

We climbed over into the front seat, and watched as the car

was shackled to the back of the lorry in front. Then my father was back behind the wheel and we were heaved away out of the main road and down a side street.

That night we put up at the Commercial Hotel. It had turned into one of those wet nights in which the rain comes down, but you cannot see it, except where it haloes the street lamps. We ate alone in the dining room, which was full of heavy furniture, with a picture on one wall of a giant stag at bay on a tall, rocky outcrop. The Virgin Mary looked down on us from the other wall, blessing us with her benign munificence. The waitress served us with whispers, pityingly, as she would a shipwrecked family. My mother clutched her handbag and poked disapprovingly at the potatoes. My father meanwhile was out in the town, and from time to time would look in on us all, his raincoat streaming with water, to report on progress in his search for a gearstick and a mechanic. His eyes were bright, his movements decisive.

"Apparently there's a man in Mallow that's got a gear stick," he said.

"Mallow," said my mother. "But that's forty miles away."

"I'll have to hitchhike, or borrow a bicycle," he said. "You'll be alright here." And with that, he had gone, vanishing into the night, a faint smell of beer lingering mysteriously in the room where he had been.

My mother organised us with smooth efficiency, bathing Tom and myself together in a deep iron bath, with water that thundered upon us from ageing taps. That night my father did not return. Instead, we saw him at breakfast, in great good humour. He told us he had found just the same kind of jeep, in a scrap-yard owned by the brother of the garda that had towed us from the junction.

"And then it was too late to get back, so I went to see a Buddy Holly film in the cinema. Quite fantastic! Packed full of blokes in leather jackets, dancing in the aisles and stamping their feet. When the music got going . . . I was in the balcony and I really thought they'd bring the whole place crashing down!"

We arrived on the third day, turning the last bend off the Ring of Kerry at dusk. Spread out below were the islands, and above us the darkening mass of the mountain, as if we were on the side of some beast, the road clinging to its shoulder. The car swerved and the brakes squealed on their drums. As my father climbed out, the driver's door slammed in the fierce wind blowing in unobstructed from America, off the ocean. All of us fell quiet. The car buffeted gently. A wall of cloud hung out over the pewter sea, split with gashes of gold, where the evening sun cut through. Squalls of rain slipped across the islands below. Outside, my father checked the map, fighting with it against the steaming bonnet of the car. For several minutes we leant with our noses pressed to the windows. The hillside was studded with white cottages and tapestried with lumpy dry-stone walls. The bay at Bealtra, with its white strand beyond, lay far below.

The door flew open and the car filled with the scent of wet bracken and sea air. My father climbed in.

"We're here," he said.

Slowly he manoeuvred the car, reversing precariously at a turning off the main road, down a narrow track, descending through ever tighter hairpin turns towards the bay. At one, the bumper dislodged a flurry of boulders and clods of earth, which bounced away across the sloping fields, scaring sheep. The hedgerows flamed with fuchsia.

We stayed in a farmhouse my father had found through a letting agent in Cork.

"Its not ideal," he said. "But it will do."

A large turf fire warmed the main room, which had low beams supporting the upstairs, where damp mattresses sat on rusting springs. A sad Christ looked down upon us as we drank soup and watched the turf fire burning in the grate.

Mother tried to do the washing up in the back pantry, where there was neither running water nor sink.

"Where's the toilet?" I asked.

"Ah," he said, vaguely.

The next morning my father announced an expedition. He'd been down on the beach early, in his gym shoes and old khaki shorts, his Panama already on in the expectation of sunshine.

"There's a path leads off the back of the beach and up into the hills," he said, interrupting our half-started breakfast in the darkened house.

"There's tea here," said my mother, pouring it out, still wrapped in her dressing gown against the morning cold.

"We could fill a hamper for the day," said my father.

"We've not found a way to get proper food yet," said my mother.

"Where's the path?" asked Tom.

"How long is it?"

"Does it really go right into the hills?" I asked.

"It runs along the edge of the bay, across the cliffs. There's probably a great view down," said my father.

I can remember us, as if in some old sepia print of imperial days, the family (for such we were then) striding up my father's path. After a turn around a tall, pointed rock that guarded the bay, the path narrowed to a well-trodden ribbon along the cliff top. We began a long and hot ascent, through a jungle of nettles and ripening blackberries, steaming in the morning sun, with a picnic hamper swaying along, carried between Tom and James, the knives and forks, the plates and glasses clinking loudly as a cacophonous background to our laboured breathing.

At the head of this small tropical valley we halted while my father lit his pipe.

"Well," he said, putting his arm lightly on my mother's shoulder. "That's about a quarter of it done."

Down below the valley shimmered, the colours bending and melting in the heat, hemmed in by broken rocks embroidered with lichens, across which lizards scurried. At the bottom of the valley stood a pile of broken stones and the shape of an empty window, and a chimney breast, leaning over.

"Come on!" said father.

The path turned across another headland, and plunged downwards through deep vegetation.

"I hope there's no snakes," said mother, picking her way carefully and from time to time glancing back to check that we were all still in view.

"There's no snakes," said father, who claimed to know these things. "Saint Patrick drove them all away." I knew this. At school there was a book with a picture in it of a fellow with long, pointy slippers, wearing a cloak and a weird hat, chasing a gang of toads and snakes down the road, while a group of peasant types looked on from the top of a round tower, with their mouths all round Os.

The path led us out through dunes onto a long strand, where the sand was white and hard and the surf from the ocean boomed, the waves sweeping up in tier upon tier of green water, the sea lumpy and distant behind. We picnicked and swam. There was no one there. My father wandered off. At around four, a party of nuns came down to the beach and hid decorously at the far end, amongst some rocks, their habits flapping in the wind, before venturing together into the edges of the ocean, their pale bodies almost encased in voluminous one-piece bathers.

At the end of the beach someone, a retired sea captain perhaps, had built his house, improbably in the shape of a ship, with its pebbledashed prow bursting from the hillside. We imagined him there, bearded like Captain Haddock from Tintin, pacing his carpeted bridge and watching the shoreline for bathing nuns.

"Come on!" cried Tom. "Ma, can we go take a look?"

She hesitated and suggested that we waited till father got back from his stroll, but Tom persisted. She asked James did he want to go, but he was buried in some book, so I set off with Tom.

At the end of the strand we turned up through the gates leading to the sea captain's house. A car stood in the drive, a great black car, low-slung, with running boards. From the house came the faintest sound of classical music, and voices speaking a foreign language.

"French!" said Tom.

The car was the most extraordinary thing.

"It's a Citroen," said Tom. "It's got no springs for the bumps. Just glides right over them on air."

Then a face appeared at the window, looking down at us, and we raced through the gate and away across the heather. When I caught up with Tom, he was crouched down in a dip in the dunes.

"French," he said again. "Dad says they've got the most beautiful women in the world!"

I watched the house closely, after that. It seemed a magic house, with the special car outside, not even just English, but French, with its beautiful women inside.

"How'd they get there?" I asked. But Tom did not know.

We lay in wait by the gravelled path that ran through the bracken, hoping for clues. Shortly a young woman emerged, who must have been the nanny, and two children our age, but smartly dressed as if for church. I was disappointed to see they looked much the same as anyone you'd see on the Ormeau Road on a Sunday. Then they all climbed into the car, and we watched as it rose on its pneumatic springs, and floated past us through the heather.

"Jesus, that's class!" I said. "D'ye think we could get ourselves invited?"

"You'd need Da," Tom said. "He could chat them up. Or

we could just go. March right up to the front door, and say 'Hullo, eh, we're the Grants from over the hill and we'd like to come in.' There's nothing wrong with us."

"I'm not so sure," I said.

We discussed what we could do as the Citroen slowly took the bend in the road and disappeared towards Caherdaniel. Unfortunately, as we talked, a herd of bulls from off the hill had slowly worked their way down towards us, and now stood there, not twenty feet away, with their heads lolling in the heat, their big glassy eyes stuck with flies, and their hooves slurping in the mud, as they moved uneasily from foot to foot, watching us.

"Garn! Piss off," shouted Tom, and lobbed a stone at the leader. It hit him on the back, and bounced off.

"Take your shirt off," ordered Tom.

"They go for red. That's what's attracting them." So I did as I was told.

Seeing this, the leading bull decided to go for a wee run, towards us. He started to lumber, and let out a bit of a hoot, and then they were all coming for us, a whole field of them, some playful, with their tails flicking to and fro as they gathered speed, the noise of their hooves growing louder all the time.

Afterwards, Tom told my mother what had happened.

"Pat just panicked," he said. "Didn't you, Pats? He started waving his red shirt and the bulls went bananas!" I nodded. Tom had shouted at me, then grabbed me away from where I stood, frozen to the spot, and hauled me up onto some high rocks, where the bulls couldn't go. We'd lain for a while, as high up as we could get, and watched the waves coming in off the ocean, against the cliffs, and the gulls wheeling. After a few minutes of mooing and scraping of their horns on the stone, the bulls lost interest and moved off.

When Tom had finished telling the tale, we realised father still wasn't there.

"Where's Da?" asked Tom suddenly. Mother passed her hand over her face, perhaps to shade it from the sun. She looked along the edge of the bay, where the dunes ran down to the beach, and up to the point, where the bulls were grazing.

"Oh." she said, a little tiredly. "He'll be somewhere."

Later that evening, when he had returned, I sat with him on the pointed rock at the entrance to our bay, while he smoked his pipe. The silence was gently broken by the steady creak of oars and we watched a curragh come out in the dusk, across the mauve-pink water, rowed fast by two men in perfect unison, towards the harbour entrance where the Atlantic came in.

"There they go," said father, almost enviously. We watched as the curragh took the first wave, and rose up steeply, the men pausing in their stroke as it tipped the first crest, disappeared from view and re-appeared with the two men in it, rowing steadily, unconcerned, out into the Atlantic swell.

That night there was a big stew, with lumpy bits of meat in it from one of the cans we'd brought with us. Outside, the sea sucked and gurgled on the stone beach.

The following day we found a way to buy bread from a farm up the hill, and fish from the pier, and a well where you could draw water, set back in a lush enclosure in the centre of a field. We even found the toilet, or at least a dark and noisome cave, where my father could erect his equipment.

On our third day there my father went to the back of the car and emerged with a paintbox, marked with the name Captain Grant and well used. We followed him as he set off for the marker that dominated the bay. My father settled himself at the foot of the marker, erected his easel and began to paint, with his eyes half closed, his pipe unlit and whistling between his teeth as he breathed, ignoring the three of us squatting there at his feet, except when one or other of us got too close. Then he lashed out with his foot.

"Get back!" he shouted. "Get back out of the way."

When the painting was done, he carried it down into the house and stood it by the narrow window to catch the last of the evening light. He looked at the painting from every angle.

"Well," he said. The painting showed the bay, the wild flowers, the marker on the reefs and the empty ocean beyond, sketched out lightly in aquarelle upon grey paper.

"That's lovely," said mother. "That's really lovely." But my father seemed faintly dissatisfied, standing first to one side, then the other, peering at it.

My father had no real friends as such, and had more or less turned his back on his wider family, but everywhere he went, perhaps because of this, he would meet ordinary people, and somehow strike up conversations. Indeed I can remember watching him, that first holiday, on the jetty, standing smoking his pipe, as a fisherman swung creels down into his boat, tied up there. My father sauntered over. I could hear his voice, loud above the cry of the gulls.

"What kind of fish have you got there?" and the reply, in impenetrable Gaelic.

"Fish!" he said loudly, gesturing with his hands to make sure he had been understood. The fisherman nodded and showed him a basket of mackerel. And soon my father was at it, bargaining and asking about the right kind of tackle, in sign language. It was only later that we discovered the man had been speaking English, but unaccustomed to the Kerry accent, my father had misunderstood him.

"What're you doing, Tom?" I asked my brother, after we'd been there a week. He was upstairs in the cottage, in his room. They'd given him one of the rooms at the end, with a narrow window that looked out over the bushes and flowers that crowded the boundary wall, out over the bay. For a few days he'd been trailing mysteriously along the beach at low tide, gathering driftwood, pieces of cork, bits of old string and fragments of things which had been so altered by the force of the sea as to be unrecognisable. Up in his room he'd now started to assemble a boat, with three masts and sails cut from greaseproof paper, with all the old wormholes in the wood sealed up with tallow from candles, and string to hold the stone keel on.

"Jesus," that's great, I said. He looked surprised at me, that anyone could think anything he did was great.

"S'just a boat," he said.

And then he carried it away down to the beach where it was high tide at the time. The pier was quiet, the barnacled stones hot underfoot, and the green water sucking up and down the side of the pier with a soft glooping noise.

"Yez'll never get it back," I said to him.

"I will so," he said. He held the boat so the sails filled with wind, making a faint flapping sound, and checked the cotton strings that held them, tied off round halves of father's old burnt-out match ends, driven into the rotten wood.

James came down too, clutching a book, to see what was going on.

"What're ye doin'?" he asked.

"Just you watch," said Tom. "This is goin' to be great."

James peered closely at Tom's boat, and I could see that he knew it wasn't going to work but wouldn't tell Tom, out of respect for his feelings.

"Could you not just keep it like, on the mantelpiece or something?" he suggested. But Tom had bent over the side of the pier, with his legs in their short trousers waving as he tried to keep his balance while the boat fell into the water with a loud splash, bobbing up a couple of feet further out. The wind filled the sails and it began to zigzag erratically away from the pier, out into the bay.

"Ah, that's goin' great," said James.

There was a bit of a silence as we tried to judge which way it was headed and where it might end up. Then it got stuck up against the side of one of the old wooden fishing boats moored in the bay.

"Ah fuck," said Tom.

"Yous'd been better with it on the mantelpiece," I said.

"It could still be OK," said James.

The boat drifted free but something now seemed to go wrong with it. Maybe it had been damaged or something by banging up against the side of the fishing boat, or maybe the wooden hull had begun to get waterlogged, because it began to go round in circles, and with each circle it began to drift further out to sea.

"Go and get Da," I said.

"Na. What'd he ever be able to do?" said James. Tom was staring at his boat, as it grew smaller, and sank deeper in the water.

"Mebbe the tide'll bring it back in Tom," I said. But he just stared at the thing impassively, as if it was what he would have expected to happen to it anyway from the first moment he set to building it.

"I'll get Da," I said, and ran away off up the pier, over the bridge, and up the muddy path to the cottage, my bare feet slipping as I went, and into the house, where mother was cleaning our gym shoes on the porch.

"Where's Da?" I asked. "Tom's boat's gone."

I hunted the old fellow down, smoking his pipe by the marker and he strolled down to the pier in his brown plastic sandals. When we got there, Tom was still standing watching his boat, circling ever further out into the bay, with its paper sails fluttering forlornly, now even lower in the water.

"Oh dear," said my father, ruffling Tom's hair for him, to make him feel better.

"That one looks a goner, doesn't it Tom." At which point Tom's boat just upended and sank without trace.

After that we all set to making boats, like it was some kind of mad race. For days on end the house was stuffed with bits of rotten wood, plastic bags, old fishing line, anything we could scavenge that'd let us have a faster boat than our brothers, and the old fellow took quite an interest, until James built a contraption three foot long that stank of fish and outsailed all of ours completely.

A couple of days after that Tom's first boat was washed back up on the beach, minus all its sails, and slathered in seaweed. I turned it over with my foot, and hid it, in case he'd find it and be disappointed.

On the way back North we fought in the car and Tom had to be put out before we'd even cleared Caherdaniel. My parents agreed to a stop in Killarney.

"Fleshpots!" my father announced, crashing the gears as he tried to ease the car into the main car park, already filled with tourist coaches. They bought us ice cream, and we bullied them into a gift shop.

"He can have this one. It's reduced." The wee pig looked out at me from its display case. It was made of black and shiny wood, and was barely the size of an adult thumbnail. The brothers had got their things: James had got himself an Irish cottage, with thatched roof, and Tom had got himself a shillelagh, which he swung round his head. Father was anxious to be off, looking at his watch and saying "Pah!" loudly at the contents of the display cases, while mother checked her purse. Eventually the pig was wrapped in paper and handed to me in a small box, and we set off.

I played with the pig as the car toiled up a long hill out of town. Though it had only three legs rather than the four that full price pigs had, it had two eyes made of pearls, and its two eyes gleamed with what seemed to be an utterly malicious little glint, as if to say, "I'm a right clever little pig."

At the top of the pass, the engine boiled over and we all climbed out onto the heather. Tom chased James over the rocks, bellowing like some kind of yahoo, while I messed about with the pig, rolling it down the sides of boulders, until eventually, by the time the engine had cooled, I'd lost the thing in a bog pool.

"For God's sake! We can't look for it now," said my father, while my mother poked helplessly in the brackish water with a stick.

"Come on!" shouted father, and picked me up and stuffed me in the car, slamming the door.

"You can wait a minute, Bernard!" protested my mother.

"We've got to get on!" he shouted, as he crashed the gears again.

At home in Belfast I shunted miniature trucks and coupled engines, filling the dead space between the end of the holidays and the start of the new school year. Down below I could hear my father crying out loud to himself as he tried to work in his study:

"No! Oh damn you, you damned fool Grant!"

Mother became wary, and moved around the house in a birdlike fashion, on tiptoe, instructing us all to silence. From time to time father would fling open his window, and shout at the neighbour's dog to be quiet. He hardly spoke at meals.

"Do be quiet!" my mother would hiss to us on the stairs. "Your father finds it so difficult to write."

One day I strayed into my father's study. He seemed almost relieved to see me.

"Hullo young man," he said, his big owlish eyes tired behind the horn-rimmed spectacles. "And what are you up to?" I hovered there, twisting on one leg, taking in his wide table awash with typewritten sheets and carbon papers, with endless markings up and scratchings out. The bin overflowed and the air was thick with the smell of old pipe smoke. I told him of the trains I planned, but he seemed far away, neither there with me, nor yet focussed on his own work and the tasks in hand.

"That's nice," he said. "That's very nice."

At supper one night James unwisely asked my father some questions about the history he was doing at school. My father in response began to take my brother aside, after meals, and I could hear him being tutored:

"So, King William was neither a constitutional, nor necessarily an unconstitutional monarch . . ." or, insistently, my father would ask him questions the meaning of which escaped me:

"So, what is Taylor's theory as to the causes of the dissolution of the monasteries, James?" My mother crept about the house, for fear of interrupting the exercise of genius, while my brother James began to stay away from meals. The house became claustrophobic.

Then the weather changed. We were all outside at Halloween. The garden was sheathed in a silver mist, which hid most of its distinguishing features. My father had lit the Catherine wheels and admired their whirling in the fog. He had allowed us to throw jumping jacks in the hedgerows and to swing the sparklers around our heads. Then he vanished into the garage, only to re-emerge with the largest rocket any of us had ever seen.

"No, its not safe, Bernard," said mother, firmly.

"Here, look, give me the matches." My father wore an old felt cap pulled over his eyes. The night had a kind of damp, seeping cold to it, and smelt strongly of gunpowder. We watched him, his hands shaking, as he lit the fuse. The pipe into which he had placed the rocket seemed to glow for a moment where he had driven it into the lawn, leaning at a sharp angle so it pointed down the drive. Then with a hiss and a burst of flame the missile took off, weaving from side to side as it accelerated across the road, down the drive of the house on the far side and against the door of the garage opposite, where it exploded in a mass of orange and green stars. The smoke drifted, thickening the mist. There was a silence. We three brothers stood in a line, watching.

"That'll teach them to let their bloody dog bark," said my father.

We knew then that our father was not a happy man.

"What do you think is wrong with him?" I asked.

"Dad?" My brother Tom turned his school cap between his fingers.

"Yeah, Dad."

"He's okay. Mum think's he's okay."

"But Mum thinks everyone's okay." This was my brother James.

"Everyone is okay," said Tom.

"But there is something wrong with him," said James

"Shut up, would you," said Tom." There's nothing wrong with Dad."

"It's Mum wants him to be a Professor," said James, seriously.

I pondered this. Would father being a Professor make things different? We visited Professors' houses, and they were much like ours. They were large, with heavy furniture, thick pile carpets and they had grand paintings on the walls. They all had children who had dolls' houses and some even had ponies and they drove large cars, and spoke in the same kind of loud, confident voices as our parents spoke. And yet, our father was not a Professor. In fact there was probably little chance of his being one now, as my mother confided in me one day.

"Oh, he's just throwing away his chances," she said. "He always did. Just couldn't get down to it. It's the family curse." I blinked, and nodded wisely.

"Tom, do you think there's a family curse?" I asked.

"Like the black claw?"

"Mum says there's a curse."

"She just means Dad. Dad's okay," said Tom, reassuringly.

CHAPTER SIX

"You're a fucking Mick, Grant,"

"A wee fucking Mick, that's what you are." They'd been dragging all the first years through the toilets, one by one, to find out if by any chance there'd been any Catholics slip unnoticed into the school.

"Fucking wee taig."

"I'm not a taig."

"Come on, sing 'The Sash My Father Wore', you wee cunt."

"I can't sing. I'm a Plymouth Brethren," I said.

"A Plymouth what?"

"Brethren," I said.

The four boys stood there, nonplussed.

"Say that again."

"Plymouth Brethren," I said clearly.

"If you ever get into any trouble, tell them you're a Plymouth Brethren," my father had said to me on my first day at the big school.

"But what am I?" I had asked him.

"You're nothing. No religion, I mean. You could say that too."

"Yes, just say 'I'm nothing', or 'Undecided', or something like that," my mother agreed.

"You're a fucking taig anyway," said the biggest boy, and kicked my ankle, to see what would happen.

"A fuckin' wee Mick. Fucking Patrick. What sort of a fucking name is that? What happened in 1690? What fucking happened in 1690?"

Then, before I could say, "King Billy whipped the Fenian scum," they gave me the answer:

"We's beat the shite outa you fuckin' Micks. That's what we done, Grant. We beat the shite outa the Micks!"

"I'm not a Mick!" I protested.

"Don't try that on us, Grant. We can tell you're a fuckin' Mick."

"How? How's can you tell?"

"Don't get fucking clever with us, Grant," they said.

"We jest know. Don't mess with the Orange boys."

"I'm no fucking Mick," I said. "I live up the Lisburn Road. My Da's Bernard Grant and my Uncle's Jim Grant. He marches on the twelfth."

I could hear the water gurgling in the toilets. A wee fellow flushed the loo down the end and banged out the door with his trousers half down, trying to run before they could get to him. But they ignored the interruption.

"Jim Grant?" One of the bigger lads recognised the name. "Didn't he marry McConochy's elder sister?"

"Lizzie," I said. "Elizabeth McConochy."

"Lizzie! Is she your aunt then?"

"Aye," I said.

"Well, by fuck why didn't yez say so? And we'd never have had none of this bother," one of them said, subsiding, and adding a bit sheepishly, "Well, anyway, just watch your fucking step, Grant, just the same."

I didn't tell my mother any of this. She'd not have understood. She'd have worried and it never seemed the right time now to bring her bad news. There was a strange atmosphere, both on the streets and at home now. It was as if everything was speeding up ever so slightly, like the beginning of some not quite pleasant ride at the fair.

During term time the big dinners started up again, but they seemed somehow different. One night the supper guests were all at it, discussing the usual; would Ireland ever change, and what the future might hold. My father pushed back his plate and asked whether anyone remembered the sad tale of the Professor of Greek? The fellows looked puzzled, and scratched their heads and some said they did and others said they didn't.

"He was the youngest chair ever at the Queen's University, and had a brilliant career ahead," said my father, but added with some satisfaction that this did not mean much since Greek was a dying tongue and no one wanted to learn it any more, particularly not in Ireland.

"But that," my father said, "Is by the by, as it is not the Professor's academic achievements that matter; but the results of his struggle against the locking of swing parks on Sundays."

Now a few of the audience seemed to recall the case, and there were cries of, "Ah yes!" and smiles or recognition all round as my father continued:

"The Professor had two young children who didn't enjoy spending Sundays in the front parlour clutching prayer books. So one particularly dull Sunday he grabbed a hacksaw and marched down to the park, past the park keeper's cottage. The park keeper unfortunately saw him passing the window with his hacksaw, put on his park keeper's hat, and followed the Professor as he marched up to the nearest swing and started sawing away at the padlock and chains. The park keeper crept up behind him, half hoping the Professor was some ordinary fellow who was short of a length of chain on a Sunday, or that there's some other reasonable explanation, but unfortunately he can see by the brown corduroys and the Hush Puppy shoes and the general manner of the fellow that something else is going on.

'Here you!' says the keeper. 'What the hell do you think you're doing?'

The Professor stands up to his full height (for this is the moment he has been waiting for) and says:

'These swings should be open on Sundays,' and soon enough the Professor of Greek is down Marlborough Street Police Station being charged with malicious damage."

At this point in the telling of the story over dinner,

my father paused for dramatic effect, with everyone chuckling, and looking forward to the end of the tale, including
me.

"Except that the Professor refuses to give his name and
address!" said my father. "So the Sergeant bangs him up for
the night, and it's all over the papers the next day, and the
Professor of Greek gets to be in the "Belfast Telegraph" and
the "News Letter" just as he hoped."

Everyone round the table nodded and said, yes, they
remembered the case, but my father said he bet they didn't
remember what happened in the end, and they said, no, they
didn't and wasn't it curious, and my father gave himself
another big belt of drink and delivered what he hoped would
be the punch line:

"Except that when the Professor's case comes to court the
magistrate, it appears, respects learning of any sort, and particularly learning of the ancient kind, and even has his son up
at the University. Not only that but he can see that the Professor's the kind of fellow that's just gagging to cause more
trouble. So he lets the Professor off scot free and the park stays
shut on Sundays." My father slapped the table. "There!" he
said. "You have it in a nutshell!"

I could hear my mother clattering about in the kitchen,
and all the types round the dinner table were set for a
good argument over their puddings, gearing up to give it the
old:

"Surely the problem isn't locked parks, but not enough
parks," or "Who'd be needing parks on Sunday what with the
luscious countryside the good Lord's given us," or, "Surely be
to God the people living next door to the parks are entitled to
a bit of peace and quiet on Sundays," arguments which are by
now familiar to me, when all of a sudden my brother James
piped up with:

"What's in a nutshell? You don't solve anything just by
giving up."

My father seemed a bit put out by this, but all the same pleased that his son's putting a view.

"But that's just it!" he said, stabbing the air with his finger, his eyes bright with the wine. "You can't do anything."

"How d'you know?" said James. "None of you's have ever tried." There was a bit of a hush and then James added: "And anyway, the parks aren't the main issue."

"Well, what is?" asked father, and I could see he was a bit angry now, but James saw he'd gone too far, and blushed and stammered, and got up and ran out of the room.

And then it got to be a regular scene; sometimes my brother would argue at breakfast too, over the toast and the tea. My father would be reading the Irish Times and thinking, frowning, and then he'd say something like:

"They'll never learn," or, "What utter tosh!" or, "They'll put us back another fifty years." My brother James would scowl.

"Back where?"

"Back to the dark ages," my father said.

And then every so often the paper would arrive on the mat with the front page showing a march, or a crowd, or a picture of someone with their head cut open, and my father and my brother James would fight to get to read it first, in the hall.

I developed a heavy frown. I lay in my room, watching the ceiling, or stretched myself out on an old trunk which I pushed against the window, and watched the street outside. The girl opposite, who was a couple of years older, began to interest me as she set off to school, in her short skirt and high heels. It seemed suddenly as if my childhood was disappearing, going far back into some space from which it could never be recalled.

Tom was now into his fourth year and travelled each day to school on the train. It was a mixed school, and he lay in his bed, describing how he had kissed a girl in his class and held her hand, or how two girls had chased him behind the cycle sheds.

"What d'you make of that, Pats?" he said. I lay, silent and envious under the covers until, frustrated by my silence, Tom leapt from his bed to land on mine, and pummelled me with his fists until my mother came into the room with a pile of clean sheets and pillowcases.

"Tom's duffing me up!" I complained.

"What do you mean, Patrick? 'Duffing up?' What kind of language is that now? I do wish you'd speak English."

Indeed it was about this time my mother intensified her campaign against the Belfast accent about the house, and against most signs of Irishness. We responded by increasing the broadness of our accents, and larding our language with as many Irishisms as we could muster, and inventing a few more.

"What are you? Are you English or are you Irish?" she asked one day.

"Irish," we chorused.

Her most successful tactic though was divide and rule, where she would pull me clear from Tom or James, away to one side.

"I will not have you using that dreadful language around the house. Now talk properly, will you."

"Ah Jasus, me arm is broke altogether, Ma!" cried Tom insolently.

"C'mon Ma, gi'us a break!" I echoed his rebellion.

Soon I began to time my departures at breakfast to coincide with the girl from across the road, hoping one day to have the courage to stand next to her in the bus queue, and perhaps even speak to her. One day I did queue up next to her, but found I could say nothing, while she gossiped away with the girl next to her, both of them in their bottle green uniforms, chattering away and laughing and joking as the drizzle came in down the mountain and up Belfast Lough, hanging in the autumn air.

"Don't be vague, shoot a taig," was scratched in the paint-work of the bus shelter. I took out my biro, and me and Peter scratched "F.T.P" alongside, while we waited for the bus. Fuck The Pope. It made me one of the boys.

We sat down the back of the top deck with the smokers, and you could cut the air with a knife. The girls stood on the bottom deck, apart from the ones from the Model School. We couldn't get our eyes off them.

"Tom'd know what to do," I whispered. "He'd be right in there with the 'Well hello girls and would you like to have a fag,' or something."

"Is that what he says to girls?" asked Peter.

"Oh aye, or 'Hullo, my name's Tom, what's yours?'"

"The best way is to ask some sort of a question where they've got to give a big long answer," whispers Peter. "So's you can engage them in conversation."

"Like what?"

"Like 'What subjects are you doin' for yer GCEs?'"

"What if they're at the Model School and not doing GCEs, Peter?"

"Yez could ask them something different." But we couldn't think of anything different to ask a girl.

The bus paused at Bradbury Place for the driver to have a smoke. In the lull we heard everyone chatting, and a few of the old biddies complaining down below as to how the driver should be doing his job and not smoking, and him shouting back at them as to how they should be keeping quiet and not moaning and let a fellow have a bit of peace. But in the chit-chat we kept hearing people saying things like, "It's getting really desperate."

Now people have been saying this about everything for years, as in, "My feet are really desperate today, or, "I'm desperate for a cup of tea," but now when they needed the word, it had somehow lost its meaning. So instead some of them said, "Aye and isn't it chronic the way the trouble goes on.

And after all haven't the Fenians got nearly everything they always wanted?" Chronic seemed to fit more exactly.

"Chronic like a cold yez can't shake off," said Peter.

Peter was a serious boy. He lent me his James Bond books: "The Spy Who Loved Me" and "From Russia with Love". His Mum was really strict; when I went round there, the house was always absolutely spotless, and if Peter so much as dropped the slightest thing on the ground she almost made him lick it up off the floor. His room was like it had been decorated by a geometry teacher, with his posters of women and monsters all neatly lined up with each other, and his pyjamas carefully folded under the pillow, as I discovered when we started to beat the shite out of each other with the pillows. Then we were chucked out onto the street by his mother, and the door slammed shut behind us till tea.

It was not the best place for hanging around as there was only a big flat field that led over to the new industrial estate, bounded by a high wire fence. Some lads were out playing football on the field, and for a while we leant in on the fence watching them. Peter pulled out a pack of cigarettes.

"Capstan full strength," he said. "These'll block your head." I smoked one with him and my head spun. I felt like I was going to be sick.

"When're you next going down to Markethill?" I asked.

"The weekend," he said. "By jeez these is strong."

He sucked the cigarette deeply and handed it back to me red hot, held upright so the last of the ash wouldn't fall off along with what tobacco was left. There was a long pause then, while I sucked the hot cigarette, finally stubbing it out against the fence, coughing as I did so.

"*This* weekend?" I asked.

"Aye," he said. "D'ye want to come?"

When we arrived the place was the same as ever, though

Peter's grandparents were even older and more stooped than I remember, though his grandmother's eyes still glinted when she saw us climbing out of the car with our bags.

After lunch we found some drink in the parlour. The cabinet was made of heavy wood, still highly polished and full of bottles, going far back.

"Here, we'll try some of this, shall we?" said Peter to me. "Gaymer's cider," he said, reading the label.

"You's could mix it with sherry to make scrumpy," I said. "That's what my Da did in the war." And so Peter took out a pair of half pint glasses and a bottle of Emva Cream and a bottle of cider, and we crept away off down the hall and out the door, with the sound of the Archers coming from the radio in the kitchen.

"Where'll we go?" I asked.

"Down the hayshed," said Peter.

So we drank a few glasses of the stuff. The cider you could just take, but the sherry you had to swallow down, holding your nose. Even mixed in, in wee doses with cider you could still taste it. Peter started looning around, like he couldn't stand up, which was true on account of the bales of hay we were sitting on, which were fresh and soft beneath us, stacked loosely about ten feet high.

Later, one of the men came into the yard in his brown jacket, with his wellingtons all smeared with cow dung and his old cap down over his face.

"Git down outa that," he said, when he caught sight of us. "Did you's not hear of the wee fellow in Dromore last month who fell in a gap between some straw bales and was suffocated to death?"

At this Peter managed to stand up and toasted him with his glass and said did he want a drink, and I saw the fellow hesitate.

"C'mon and take a drink," Peter repeated.

I saw the old fellow hesitating some more.

"Sherry," said Peter.

"Oh no, now Peter, I'd never be touching sherry."

"Go on, just a wee drop."

"I've the chickens to see to," he said. "Anyhow, how come you's boys have got the sherry?"

"Granny give us it," said Peter.

"Well, if I wez you's, I'd lay offa that sherry," said the man and made off to the henhouse, leaving us there with the starlings swooping in and out of the eaves of the barn.

"Shall we go get Elaine?" said Peter, in the end.

"Aye," I said, and we hid the drink in amongst the bales and slid down to the ground.

And then, trailing half drunk across the fields towards her house, we heard a volley of shots, and the leaves on the trees behind us were ripped by passing bullets.

"Fuck it. She's fucking mad," said Peter. I dropped down to join Peter where he had thrown himself in the undergrowth. The shooting stopped, and Elaine came down over the fields towards us, laughing like mad. She was a good bit older now, and she seemed to dance over the grass with an easy step, the rifle under one arm.

"What're you doing in the ditch like that, Peter?" she said, as Peter pulled himself out of the bracken. She nodded at me in recognition, as we both stumbled upright.

"This is Da's new gun. He's got it in case the IRA come for him," she said, and laughed again, showing off the new rifle, turning it over in her hands. "It's a .22. Here, look at this."

She reached into the pocket of her coat and pulled out a handful of shells, which she fed into the magazine. Then she clipped the magazine shut, pointed the gun at the tree-tops where the crows were nesting, and let rip six or seven shells with a violent, pumping action, the gun spewing empty cartridges out at our feet. The trees erupted into a cloud of feathers and the crows flapped angrily into the darkening sky. There was a short silence.

"Let's have a go," said Peter, and took it in his hands. She took another handful of bullets, and showed him how to load. Peter was less certain in his firing, and shot perhaps three shells off before pausing.

"Jeez," he said. "That could do some damage."

We messed around for an hour or two, shooting holes in cans and smashing bottles on the high wall in the orchard, till the ammunition ran out and we had to go in for supper. It was that interesting, I'd never much time to notice that Elaine was a girl and I'd spoken to her to say:

"How d'ye do this?" and, "Is this how yez take the safety catch off," and, "Fuck me, that feller is blasted full o' holes," when we rescued one of the cans that'd been ripped to bits by our shooting.

After supper, we met again, waiting like children in the long grass outside her house until she could come out. The night was cool, and unnaturally clear. The stars shone, very far up. There was a sense of breathless space, and of a particular still and heady silence. We whistled, to let her know we were waiting, and saw her changing through an upstairs window. Then the kitchen door in the house slammed, and she came running out through the long grass to meet us.

We went down to the chicken run to see if we could find the fellow from the afternoon to tease some more, retrieving the cider along the way. We crept into the hen coop, where the chickens were roosting, their soft murmurings peaceful, and the smell of their droppings heavy in the warm air under the lights. For a moment we stood in awkward silence.

"Have ye heard about hypnosis?" I said. It was something I'd read, some foolish story, that you could hypnotise a chicken. She stood beside me, very close.

"What's that?"

"Hypnosis. Hypnotise a chicken."

Then Peter started up with an imitation in the deepest and most intractable of South Armagh accents:

"Yar' not goin' till 'ipnotoize onny chuckens of mine," he said. She giggled.

"Here, you," I said, and tried to catch a bird, but it fluttered heavily away before I could get to it.

She laughed again, and advanced down the henhouse behind me, with her hands held out. I drew a line in the dust on the floor, and laid a piece of old string along it.

"Here's what you need," I said.

"I'll get you's a bird," she said. Suddenly she jumped forward and grabbed one, the others rising up in a cacophony, stirring dust and a cloud of feathers. As the dust and the noise subsided, she came towards me, clutching the bird.

"Show me," she said, holding the bird against herself. I took the bird, and my hand touched hers for a moment. The bird began to struggle and kick and to fight and I forced its head down onto the single line I'd lain in the dust, so that one eye looked out one way and the other eye the other. The legs scrabbled, the claws cutting my hands, and then the bird was completely still, as if hypnotised, one eye looking out each side of the line.

I stood back, and took my hands away from the bird's neck. The bird stayed as it was, completely still, with its eyes unfocussed. We hesitated, all of us, looking at the bird, expecting it to spring to life. Gently, we moved its head, sideways, but found that it was dead.

"It's fucking dead, you pillock," said Peter. So we jammed it upright in the mesh, to make it seem alive, so there'd not be trouble.

The next morning I was desperate to see her again, but Peter lingered over his bacon, eggs and tea. I pressed him to go back up to where she lived, but he said he'd to see to the horses that morning.

"Can't you just do it quick?" I said. His eyes narrowed, as if he'd worked out what I was after.

★

When I got back to Belfast it was to find my parents in James' room. My father was moving the mattress off the bed, while mother filled a big trunk with lining paper, then shirts and books, socks and pants, all neatly washed and stacked. Outside the window the first of the Autumn mists was creeping in.

"What are you doing? Are we swapping rooms or what?" I asked.

"Where's James off to?" They paused, my mother and father, in their preparations.

"James is going away," said my mother. "Away to study. He has been given a great opportunity, Patrick." I could not imagine what kind of opportunity required such a total clearance.

"Come on," said my father. "Give us a hand with the trunk, would you?" Slowly, we bumped the trunk down the stairs and out into the hall, and then my father backed the car up to the front door. On the steps he turned and said to me:

"James is going to Oxford."

"To visit?"

"To study," said my father, as if it were a punishment.

At first I felt excitement as the car turned by the Albert Clock, towards the docks. We were all squeezed in as the trunk had taken most of the space, with my brother there between us, wearing a tie, slightly askew, the laces already undone on his tight, highly polished shoes.

We helped him up the gangplank, found his cabin, stowed his luggage, and then climbed back down to the quayside to watch the boat go. I stood there amongst the crush of men in damp gabardines, and girls sobbing and waving, and watched for his figure at the rail. My mother peered upwards.

"Is that him there? Oh Bernard, is that him?" Then Tom spotted him, with his coat collar drawn up, at the back of the second class, leaning over the side.

"There he is!" he shouted. "Look, Ma, he's smoking a cigarette!"

This was good news, as it breached the sadness we'd all been holding in. It was something that took our minds off it.

"The stupid boy," said father, lighting his pipe.

The crowd on the quay was something considerable. There were boats to Ardrossan, to Glasgow, to Liverpool, to the Isle of Man, and the last one out at night to Heysham, that my brother sailed upon. One by one, their mournful siren blasts echoed along the river, as they slipped their moorings, the noise deafening us.

At last my brother's boat was untied, and a gap opened between quay and ship, my brother waving, as the propellers turned and the smoke drifted across the oily river. His figure shrank, slowly at first, then faster as the ship gathered speed downriver, until he was lost to view amongst the blur of faces at the rail. We always waved in our family until you could no longer see.

"Why've they sent James away?" I asked Tom later.

"It's what happens when you're clever." said Tom. "So you'd better watch out."

"Why's he gone to Oxford?"

"It's where clever people go, you thicko. You know, where Da went wrong."

But after James's departure, the home seemed emptier, and quieter. His bedroom had been cleaned and aired, the walls redecorated, though on mother's orders he'd left his record collection. Along with the Beatles, the Searchers, the Drifters and the Beach Boys, he also had a bit of an Irish collection, as me and Tom discovered when we went through what was left of his stuff, to see if there was anything worth having. We passed a pleasant enough hour playing his records, the house echoing to "Yellow Submarine" and some of the old Irish numbers by the Dubliners and Tom Clancy. When we played these, we could hear in the background all the fellows having a grand time, cheering and clapping and singing out, "Good on ya!," so we turned the volume up as loud as we could, till the speakers rattled with the "Croppy Boy" and you could hear it outside in the street, with the neighbours looking up at the open window till we were all thoroughly cheered up. That is until father came in and pulled the plug out of the wall and told us all to stop that bloody racket and wasn't it bad enough James having left his Fenian songs in the house without people going and playing them like a crowd of yahoos.

CHAPTER SEVEN

A few days after James's departure we found my father out in the drive alongside the house with a small blue dinghy on a trailer, exchanging five pound notes with the owner of the boat and being shown the varnished spars and the ropes. He insisted on having the sails erected there and then, in the driveway, and spent the evening happily walking around it, puffing on his pipe and adjusting the trim, until mother told him to come in and put the damned thing away for the night. The next morning he'd cancelled his lectures and was away off with the car to a welder's in east Belfast, getting a towbar fitted, and then after lunch he was down the road with the boat and all of us shoved in the back of the car, to watch the launch.

"Where are we going?" we asked. "Strangford Lough," he said. "It's all arranged. I've joined a club down there. There's a slipway a mile or two off the road. There's a clubhouse too." It was like a great escape he'd been planning for months.

On the slipway, he ordered us all out to help, and produced a set of life jackets from the boot, smelling of salt, old age and over-use. He'd acquired a huge nautical vocabulary, as if he'd been reading up on it all secretly, in his room at night.

"Tighten up on the mainstay!" he shouted. "Give us that batten, will you Pat. Who's got the jib?"

By the time the dinghy was launched it was already late afternoon. Carefully he loaded us all into the boat, then took the commanding position next to the tiller, and slowly we sailed around the moorings. There was a look of supreme contentment on my father's face, tinged with a little anxiety and self-consciousness, as we turned erratically around the stern of this or that large yacht, named "Castlemaine" or "Clonakilty," my father bellowing "Ready about!" and

"Lee-oh!" and the yacht owners laughing (or so it seemed) at our progress.

When we got home father seemed in a better mood than I'd seen him for years.

"Well," he said. "That's certainly blown away the cob-webs."

"It's a pity poor James wasn't there to enjoy it," said mother. But the old fellow said nothing.

James existed for us now mainly in the form of letters, which were read aloud at the breakfast table, where we listened in for news of him.

"Dear Mum and Dad," my mother read. "I have settled in quite well at Magdalen College, and have a good room, though the place is full of toffs and snobs. I have joined the Socialist Society and met up with Seamus Riordan and some other lads from home. In the end I don't think I'll stick with history, though. The big thing here seems to be to study PPE which is much more my kind of stuff; politics, philosophy and economics. Money is very tight. At the weekends we hang around the transport cafes as they're the best place for a cheap bite, and you get to meet some amazing characters." She paused. As she read, her tone had altered to one of disapproval.

"What does it mean?" she asked. "He had enough money when he left. Why doesn't he eat in college?"

"And who on earth is Seamus Riordan?" asked father. We sat on the edge of our seats, Tom and I, thrilled at the news of James's decline.

I dreamed of phoning Elaine myself. Once I'd even got into the hall and dialled half the number when my mother came in and said she needed the phone. After that I lost the courage of the moment. I agitated to get Peter to take me again to

Markethill. I invited him sailing, before the weather turned cold and the boat was laid up for the winter. But no invitation came. I worried they'd found the chicken; that we'd been reported; that I'd never get to go there again. I asked him questions all the time about her and suffered at night, trying to sleep. And then I realised too much time had passed for a phone call to be reasonable, and for the moment she became a distant fantasy.

Then one morning in December I came downstairs and found a couple of old plastic bags in the hall, stuffed with clothes, left on the chair by the phone, and the house full of the smell of cigarettes. James was back from England, and the kitchen full of frying. But the dining room, where you might've expected chat and laughter was silent. I went in there and found my brother leaning across the table with the Irish News out, spread right across one end of it and an ashtray out beside him. My father was at the other end of the table, puffing away on his old pipe, and I could see he'd been up early because the ashtray was already full of a stack of old pipe emptyings and burnt-out matches.

"Hi, James," I said. "We were expecting you last week."

"Hullo, Pats," he said, looking up. "How're you doing?" I noticed he'd broken the frame of his spectacles and fixed it with sticking plaster.

"He missed the boat," said father.

"How's can you miss a boat?" I asked.

"God knows how he did it," said father.

James kind of tutted and ran his hand through his hair, and returned to reading his paper.

"I mean you'd think at his age he'd be able to catch a boat," said father, to the top of James's head.

Then mother came in with some more bacon, busying around with her apron on, and shifting James's ashtray to one side quietly and putting the plate down so as not to disturb his reading, though when he picked up the knife and fork, she sat down right beside him and said:

"So, tell me about the money, James. We were very worried you know."

James looked a bit scared then, I could see. I could see he didn't really know how or why he'd got through all the money, that it was one of those revelations that had come unpleasantly to him, along with his freedom.

"There was this fellow in my economics tutorial," he said. "He reckoned that if you doubled your bets after every loss you'd never lose on the horses."

"Oh James," said mother. "That's the kind of idea that might work if you'd far more money than we have."

"That's right," said James. "I was nearly there, but needed another thousand to make it work."

"Well," said father. "Its all gone now," and with that he got up out of his seat and went up to his study, while James mooched about reading the paper, and doing the crossword and smoking cigarette after cigarette. Eventually mother came in and asked James did he not have any work to do, and when were the next exams? Then she said she was worried he'd lost the best trousers she'd given him, and why hadn't he brought any books home for the holidays? In the end James also went out of the door, banging it after him, and afterwards my mother cleared the table and opened the windows to let the smoke out.

The year turned. James left in a miserable, cold January of sleet and icy rain, and his letters became infrequent and then stopped more or less completely. At Easter he sent us a card that he was working, canning peas in Lincolnshire. Then spring gave way to summer and at last I found myself invited once more to Markethill, Peter's mother no doubt preferring her son's absence, albeit in my company, to his bored presence through the long holidays to come.

It was a very hot day in June when I next walked up towards Elaine's house. All day a heavy thunderstorm had lingered over county Armagh. Everyone was on the lawn when we reached the house, scattered around in chaise longues, wearing dark glasses and bathers. Her father was broad chested and red all over. He'd a big jug of melting ice on the table beside him, along with tonic and a bottle of gin. Elaine's sister and her brother were there, and the grandparents, half asleep in a big swing chair with a shade built over it. The boy was listening to the football, Linfield v Glentoran. Elaine was already tanned. I'd heard they'd been in Spain. It was the first time I'd seen her like that in a swimsuit and I could hardly speak.

"Hi," she said.

"Hullo," I said.

There were two cars drawn up in the long drive. Her mother got up.

"Elaine. Would ye's for God's sake get these fellows a cool drink and somewhere to sit down."

Elaine grimaced behind her mother's back and slipped away back to the house.

"Give her a hand there boys, would ye's," her mother said.

The house was large and modern, in a utilitarian sort of way, with double glazed windows and a mock Edwardian door. In the hall there was a mess of old fishing tackle and some more sunbeds stacked up alongside the riding boots and the wellingtons.

"Peter, would ye's get those," Elaine said. I followed her into the kitchen.

The kitchen felt cooler. It was on the side of the house away from the sun. Elaine smiled at me, and bent in the fridge to rootle around for ice. I filled a jug with water from the tap, and held it out to her while she tried to break the ice cubes out.

There was an awkward silence.

"Friggin' things never friggin' come out," she said.

I stood very close to her. I could see her skin, smooth and brown, and her long, confident forearms. She brushed her hair away from her face.

We lay out on the chaise longues, out in the sun. Elaine poured out the drinks from the jug we'd brought out. When she brought mine over she very slowly tipped the glass, until the icy water splashed lightly over me.

"There you are," she said. "That'll cool you down."

Later, when Peter had gone to bed, I found I could not sleep. My bedroom window was open, the net curtains blowing in on the night breeze. The countryside seemed to teem with life; strange bird cries and lowings, the easing of horses in their stables. I crept down into the kitchen, where the clock ticked and the cats stirred curiously in their baskets, stretching, expecting breakfast. What would she be doing? On the mantelpiece were photos of the grandparents as youngsters, on horseback on the great sweep of the gravel drive, with servants out on the steps.

I pulled on my trousers and my boots, and cut off up the path towards Markethill, not intending anything specific, but full of a terrible restlessness. I stopped outside the gate and looked up at her window. All the other lights were out. I could hear the faint sounds of music. Then, as if sensing my presence, as if subject to the same restless urges as me, she came to the window, and leaned out to take the night air perhaps, or to escape the heat of the house. I coughed, and saw her peering at where I stood.

"Peter?" she hissed.

"S'Pat," I whispered back. My lips were dry. In the end she came down, letting herself out through the kitchen noiselessly, then running away across the lawn to the gate.

"What're yez up to? Where's Peter?"

"Peter's asleep," I said. She seemed to take this in. She smiled at me.

"Well," she said. "Where'll we go? What'll we do now?"

"Let's walk down to the orchard," I said.

"Okay."

"I couldn't sleep," she said.

"Me neither."

"I was listening to music."

"Aye."

The orchard seemed dark and threatening, mauve in the moonlight. Suddenly, she held my hand and kissed me, against the orchard wall, her breath hot in my mouth.

"Don't tell him. He'll be mad jealous," she said.

"He's your cousin."

"Doesn't stop him fancying me, though, does it?"

Back home in Belfast I found my parents pottering in the garden, and Tom tinkering with a new motorcycle in the garage, oil flooding the floor. I longed to tell someone, but feared that doing so would somehow threaten what had started. I tried to ring Elaine, but now there was no reply. Instead I lounged about, carping, unable to concentrate on anything, watching my parents at their digging and pruning.

In our garden there was a particular division of labour, that I began to notice at that time. The garden was a fair size, with a section at the front, but also up the side and round the back of the house and a kitchen garden alongside the garage too, so there was a fair amount of work involved. Although we had Mrs Cross more or less full time inside the house we couldn't pay for a fellow to do the outside, so my mother and father did it between them; my mother would buy the plants from McGready's rose garden up by the railway line, and my father would dig the holes and then she'd put them in with the mulch. And then it would be my father that would do the pruning, out there with the secateurs, cutting bits off here and there. He'd only need a spare moment, when he wasn't playing patience or reading the newspapers, and then he'd be wandering around with the secateurs, snipping and cutting.

One day my mother let out a great shriek, and rushed out of the house after him crying out:

"No! Don't cut that one off," as he reached out with his snippers to lop off a branch that seemed a bit lopsided or insufficiently budded, except that here he seemed to have lost his head completely and had hacked one of mother's new plants right back to the root.

And then this scene became a regular little cameo, with her carefully bedding things down in the garden, or tying them to trellising so they'd get the sun and flower, and himself hacking and digging things up for the compost or the bonfire, often things that'd been in for only a week or two, that she'd bought.

And then, in their usual way of things, they'd make a wee joke about it, sitting in their chairs at the end of the day.

In August, with the summer wearing on, they took us picnicking on the boat. It was a calm day and the aquamarine waters of the Quoile were gently stirred by a light, but steady breeze which drove us down the estuary against the tide, the water gurgling and trickling under the stern. Followed by a lone seal and looped by stray gulls, we sailed out into Strangford Lough, where the sea opened up, and the flat land almost faded away at the horizon.

My father sat at the stern, holding the tiller with one hand and sucking at his pipe, while mother guarded the picnic in the middle, and me and Tom passed the time by bickering and fiddling with the ropes.

Around lunchtime we picked on one of the islands in the Lough, and brought the boat in slowly amongst the rocks and seaweed on the lee shore, my father ordering Tom out to catch the boat before we struck. There was a bit of a business getting mother off with the lunch, with the old fellow shouting away angrily at Tom who'd another idea of the right way to go about things. In the end we were all on land, the boat tied to a big boulder and the picnic blanket laid out in a sheltered spot where you could see the sea.

We ate sausage sandwiches, looking at the clouds as they drifted overhead in the clear blue sky, and watching the coloured sails of the other boats in the distance, bunching together as they raced around the buoys at the head of the Lough. No one came near us, and we were almost together there for a minute or so; my father lying down, using my mother's stomach as a pillow, and murmuring away earnestly, discussing James and the absence of letters from him no doubt. Meanwhile Tom and I searched for gulls' eggs amongst the stones, with Tom complaining all the time about the lack of girls, and then the sun went in.

Returning home the wind blew up and we reefed in the sails. The water sprayed over us. My brother Tom took the helm, handling it well, taking the boat close to the wind when the squalls blew up, and slipping the mainsheet to spill wind if ever we were close to turning over. I could see my father was pleased that Tom had learned to sail so well, and pleased that he'd not to bark out orders, or worry that things wouldn't go right.

On the way home in the car he hummed, and puffed on his pipe. But when we turned off the Downpatrick Road to go down into the city, there was a heavy pall of smoke hanging over the mountain. At first it seemed like a freak cloud, darker than the rest, rising up under the shadow of Cave Hill.

"What's that?"

My mother and father peered through the windscreen.

"It's some sort of fire."

By the time we turned into Cultra Avenue, the cloud was darker and larger, and seemed much nearer now we were back on the west side of the city. The neighbours were out on their doorsteps, talking, holding their evening papers, which showed all across the front page and in the inside pages scenes of the City ablaze. I ran upstairs to my attic window, and pulled it down as far as I could before leaning out to look over the plane trees and the grey slate rooftops to the green mountain beyond, now almost obscured. I leaned out and listened. Carried by the summer wind, just audible above the rustling of the leaves, I heard the sharp crackle of gunfire.

I rang Elaine, and this time she answered.

"How're ye doin'?" On the phone, without her presence, without having seen her, we were strangely formal.

"Where' ve yez been?"

"Greece. 'Bin on holiday." There was a pause.

"You fellows have been letting rip up there while we were away," she said.

"S'nothin'," I said. "Sure its all quietened down now."

This much was true for the moment; the city, stunned, had fallen back into a kind of awkward lull, a not quite pleasant sense of exhausted surprise, beneath which there lay the knowledge that this was not to be the end.

"I seen the pictures on the telly," she said. "I seen the pictures of the fighting."

"So what's it like down with you?"

She laughed. "Ach God, Da's shitting himself the IRA'll come up and get him." She laughed, as if it were a ridiculous idea.

"Are ye's comin' up to Belfast?" I asked.

"I'd like to," she said. My mind raced. To do what? When? How? I'd thought of nothing.

"Fuck," I hissed at myself, under my breath. How could I be so stupid?

"When're yez next down with Peter?"

"I dunno," I said. "Dunno if my mother'll let me."

The troubles were annoying as no one was sure what exactly you could do, and it was up to a few brave grown-ups to find out if you could go from Belfast to Markethill and back without difficulty, although my mother took the view that any journey into the country was likely to prove lethal under the circumstances.

"We've a hunt ball on," Elaine said. "You could come up with Peter."

CHAPTER EIGHT

When school restarted my mother rang to check that it was safe for me to go. Distractedly, she kissed me, before I set off. Outside everything appeared the same, except that when we were at the bus stop two Land Rovers came past full of soldiers armed with automatic weapons. As their vehicles droned by they looked back at us, blankly nonchalant, hiding the strangeness of it all behind fixed stares. No one said anything in the queue. It was getting that way; that you didn't speak. If you said you were surprised, it might have been misconstrued.

Then the girl from over the way came down for her bus, crossing the road carefully on her high heels, followed by Peter with his big leather schoolbag.

"Jesus, Pats, the place is crawlin' with the military," he said. "Da says they've took half of the Royal Avenue for barracks."

I thought quickly here. You could say:

"Aye and about time too." Or you could say, "No good will come of British soldiers on Irish streets." You could even say, "Thank the Lord for that and it'll get us all some peace." But the bus came before I'd decided what to say. Instead, once we were on the bus, I said to Peter:

"Jesus she's got that short skirt on again, Peter."

Father took the army's arrival strangely. For one who enjoyed the confident prediction of disaster, its appearance left him disorientated. At first he lectured loudly at supper, larding his argument with examples from his experience of counter-intelligence in Greece during the war. I could see the events disturbed him, that there was something in our predicament that he had seen before. Later on, he fell into silence, turning the pages of the paper methodically on the table at supper, as if fruitlessly seeking good news.

"What's going to happen?" Everyone asked, but no one knew. For a few days, the city fell quiet. Then Tom's school report arrived, distracting the family.

He was summoned to my father's study to discuss what was to be done. He grinned widely as he went in.

"This is it, Pats," he said. Again I overheard my father's voice, lecturing sternly, then the voices lowered and I heard Tom talking, and the unexpected sound of laughter. Downstairs in the living room my mother was knitting silently.

"How did it go?" I asked Tom, as he passed me on the landing.

"Go? Great!" whispered Tom. "Pats, they're sending me away to sea!" His whole face beamed, and he skipped to the head of the stairs, and bounded down them, three steps at a time. Down below, I overheard my mother paraphrasing the reasons to him again, and more perhaps, to herself.

"We thought it would be just the right thing to do in the circumstances," she said. "And you do love sailing. You've got a real aptitude for it, Tom, haven't you? You'll look so smart in a uniform. So smart!"

I felt overcome with envy, and sadness, fearful too with the knowledge that the house would be empty except for myself and mother and father.

"Well, that's that then," I heard my father say to himself, as if surprised at how easy it had been, as if someone else had somehow miraculously taken responsibility.

Later, he slipped downstairs to the garage and returned to his study clutching pliers and a length of wire. I was curious that perhaps he was fashioning some consolation for me, or some gadget for Tom that he might need at sea, some cunning, pleasurable object for both or either of us. But at the same time I knew in my heart that this could not be the case.

That night, after he had settled in front of the television, I looked in my father's study. That he had not been working was evident. The desk was strewn with paper, but the paper was yellowed at the edges, and the typewriter keys were covered in a layer of fine dust. The books on the shelves, leather bound, seemed part of some museum of past hopes and aspirations. Standing in the middle of the desk however was a strange and wonderful structure, a figure of a man, or half a man, made from wire, wearing a tricorn hat, delicately poised on one foot, stepping forward airily into a space with nothing in it. The wires were linked by a finely tied network of cotton thread, and the whole had only just been finished, because the pliers and the wire lay beside them on the table, and the smell of fresh pipe smoke hung in the air.

By the time Tom left, they had taken off the boat to Ardrossan, and the boat to the Isle of Man, so the quayside was not so full, and we had not so long to wait for the Liverpool boat to sail. But the departure was no easier to bear.

My mother worked for weeks, sewing and mending. She'd been sent a lengthy list of items that Tom needed. Into the house came sun hats, brass buttons, epaulettes of various kinds, mess jackets, whites, browns and blues, corduroys and dungarees, piping, gym shoes, formal shoes, deck shoes, indeed every single thing that a merchant navy officer cadet could conceivably require. These she packed into a new and multi-layered trunk, bending low to place the most valuable objects nearest the bottom where they could not be stolen en route, while my father hovered, picking up this or that item, and remarking:

"Huh!" or "Well, well," as he watched, and patting Tom on the shoulder as if he were still a small boy.

In the days before he left I would find Tom at the top of the house, reading girlie magazines, and smoking, with his new naval jacket buttoned up around his chest.

"Get a load of this one," he said. A girl, not unlike Elaine, pouted from the pages.

When he had gone, a kind of cold seemed to fill the house,

insidiously, as if coming up from the cellar. It was as if the air was growing stale, no longer stirred by Tom's sudden leaps and bounds, his headlong dives up or down the stairs. Unexpected sounds became rarer; now I knew the hour at which father's music would go on. Uninterrupted, Mahler would drone and shriek from the living room. In Tom's room, the smell of his last cigarette still lingered. I flicked through the pages of his magazines, feeling a huge erection stirring. Desperately, I smoked in the attic till the air was thick.

Peter came over.

"What's she doin'?" I asked him.

"I heard ye wez ringin' her," he said.

"I was not," I lied.

"She's a fine girl," he said.

"Aye," I said, noncommittally.

"I heard yez are coming down fer the hunt ball."

"Does she want me to?"

"Aye, she does."

James's room was the worst. Father had begun to store his junk in there. There was the old sofa on its back with the springs coming out, and the camping equipment, dusty and unused for years now, piled on his bed.

With both brothers away, there was almost nothing to interrupt the track my father had set himself upon. Quite suddenly he shovelled all his papers and books to one side of his study, bought himself a large quantity of hardboard and house paint, and retired upstairs. He listened to classical music all day. I went in and looked at him as he painted, his face calm and contented, humming along as he experimented with scraping paint, using pieces of broken protractor as a guide. Strange abstract figures, like the small wire man would erupt onto the hardboard, at first light, dancing and airy, like fairy figures, in extraordinary shades of Irish grassgreen.

"What're you doing, Dad? What's that?" I asked him. But

he sucked his teeth, and hummed, not hearing, or answered vaguely:

"It's just a little idea I'm working on."

Then he began to cut scenes from the newspapers and to subdivide them into squares with carefully ruled lines, laboriously transcribing the pictures of riots and demonstrations to the large hardboard sheets he worked upon, embellishing them, and darkening the borders with heavy slashes of colour; with reds and blacks and oranges.

When the time came at last to go to the hunt ball, we were delayed on the way by some army roadblocks and a burning lorry outside Portadown, so everything was in full swing when we arrived. The army were everywhere, or so it seemed. As we turned off the road up the long drive to the grandparents' house, two light armoured cars came down, driving very fast, with a small British flag flying from each of their radio aerials.

"There they go!" said Peter's father.

We dropped over to Markethill, where Elaine's parents were to give us a lift the rest of the way. They were both in evening dress, and well steamed up before we even started. I'd never seen Elaine in a dress. I'd assumed she'd wear jeans, sandals, one of those old mauve T-shirts that were the style, with her hair loose like when we'd been down in the country before. She was not recognisable at all, with her hair back, and a tight silk evening dress, as she drifted over the lawn to her parents' car.

"Hiya," she said. I felt sick just to look at her as she climbed in beside me, the car filling with her faint scent.

For the dance they'd taken over some farm buildings on a big estate up the back of Armagh and decked them out well enough, with bunting and flowers. There was a big crowd there as we arrived; cars being marshalled in the field alongside and every generation there, the grandparents in their long dresses and their dinner jackets, the teenagers mostly in their smart trousers and low-cut tops. Elaine's father was in a great mood, snapping and cursing at the other drivers, and saying:

"Well, would you look at the rig up of that feller," while her mother fretted over her make-up and the risk of the car sticking in the mud of the field.

But when I got inside, I could see things were not going to go my way. There was a big crowd around the bar, which'd been set up down one end of a long barn, and at the other they'd the band, belting out cover numbers of The Beatles and country and western music. Within a second there were two lieutenants from the Royal Fusiliers all over Elaine, buying her drinks, asking her to dance, giving her smooth chatter and flattery, as I saw it, before I'd even got a drink in my hand. I could not dance. I could hardly speak.

Seeing my predicament, her father came up and put a pint of Guinness in my hand and winked at me, and nodded at the crowd and said:

"That's a grand sight now, isn't it," and replenished my glass whenever he could. Elaine danced and the band played. From time to time she glanced back at me. The floor was slippery underfoot, but with some Guinness inside me, my spirits lifted. She came over, right up to me and said:

"C'mon and have a dance,"

"If you're not busy," I said.

"Ach," she said, poking me in the chest. "I love it when you fellows get jealous."

We danced a little, before she span away to dance again with someone else, as if she had asked me there to have me feel this.

On the way back we travelled with her parents, and Peter in the car. The lieutenants followed. We could hear their patrol behind us, most of the way and see the lights, like frog's eyes, following us. Then they turned off.

"So are you doing your A levels now," asked Elaine's mother from the darkness.

"Yes."

"What're you studying?"

"French, History and English. I've just started."

"Hear that, Elaine? There's a fellow with some sense."

"Are ye goin' to University?"

"Yes."

"Trinity? That's where Peter's off to, aren't you Peter?"

"Aye, Dublin," said Peter.

"Over the water, probably," I said.

The derelict gatehouse swept past and we bumped up the track, to be dropped back at the grandparents' house. A rabbit, startled by the headlights, hesitated in the glare. Elaine's father stopped the car for a moment to watch.

"If I'd me gun I'd blast the wee fucker," he said.

Then the rabbit lollopped off in amongst the brambles that lined the road.

"Law? Did you say you'd be doing law, Patrick?" asked the mother. I said I hadn't thought what I'd be doing but I'd heard you could do politics.

"Now what kind of good is that at all," said her mother. Elaine touched my hand, gently in the dark. Peter stared straight ahead. The car stopped. All the lights were off in the old house as we climbed out and thanked them and said what a great night it had been.

"I'll see you's later," said Elaine, and their car pulled off up the drive and away, leaving me and Peter there on the road. Peter belched. It didn't seem right to go in just yet. It was as if there was business we both had to have finished. He kicked away at the gravel, scuffing his toes in it, then stooped to pick up a few pieces of stone, and threw them at the bushes, one by one.

> O, Sullivan John, you won't stick it long,
> For your belly will soon get slack,

he sang softly, without explanation. Then added gloomily:

"Not many girls though, Pat."

The song had a tragic, miserable, drunken edge to it. The crows stirred in the night treetops. His grandmother's lights came on.

"That was a fucking dirty trick," he said. He leant his back against the crumbling garden wall, and slid down it until he was sitting on the gravel.

"A fucking dirty business indeed. Jesus Christ, Pat, I'm fucked."

He pulled out a cigarette, and tried to light it.

"Peter!" came a voice. The front door opened, and we could see from the darkness the figure of his grandmother, in her nightdress, with her old housecoat draped over her shoulders, peering out short-sightedly.

"Whooooo! Tre-whit, tu-whoooo!" He stifled a laugh.

"Peter!" said the old lady, more sharply this time, then, unable to see anything, she closed and bolted the door, muttering to herself. Peter hauled himself upright.

"Lets go to the pond. Let's get Elaine and go to the pond," he said.

"You daft bastard, I'm not going to any pond at this time of night," I said.

"Bring Elaine with us, eh."

"What d'you mean?"

"Aha."

"Aha, what?"

"Aha, nothing," he said, defensively.

Then we heard a car coming down the path from the village, its lights momentarily illuminating the valley and the woods beyond. The lights came round the bend in the road, then the engine and the lights were cut and the car rolled down to a standstill opposite us, not twenty feet away, its driver invisible in the darkness.

"Whassat?"

"S'Elaine," said Peter. "You go."

"Na. You come too."

"Na. Tired. You go."

"Peter's not coming," I said, climbing in when she opened the door.

She drove off, and offered me a cigarette, chucking the packet into my lap. She was still wearing her dance outfit of the velvet dress, but with a jumper pulled over the top and her hair tucked down inside. She'd her sleeves rolled up, and smoked with one hand as she steered with the other, careering down the drive like she was running away from something, though she didn't look back.

"If you's drive fast the bumps don't get to ye's," she said.

"Where are we's going?" I asked.

"Let's go over to the mountains," she said.

"The Mournes?"

"Aye."

"Fine," I said.

I smoked cigarette after cigarette as we drove. The lights illuminated bugs, which splashed against the windscreen. We drove for miles across Armagh, without meeting anyone. The hedgerows seemed dense, and somehow all encompassing, closing in the road from the countryside around.

It was pitch dark when we stopped in Hilltown, just short of the barracks.

"Let's walk around a bit," she said. "I'm wrecked with the driving." And then she stretched and shook out her hair. The town was completely shut. It was four in the morning. I held her hand as we walked, Elaine still in her gold dance shoes.

"Did yez ever walk in the Mournes?" I asked her.

"Yer joking," she said. "Me Da's never done any exercise in his life. They never do." The main street was painted in pastels, now turned to shades of purple. She did a few dance steps, down the middle of the road, and I joined her in a clumsy waltz.

"Yer not much of a dancer."

"Na," I said. "Spatially inept. That's what my Da says."

"Spatially what?"

"Inept."

There was a silence. And then we began to laugh, I don't know why.

"I like walking at night," she said, and I slipped my arm around her waist. There was a very faint, soft breeze off the Mourne Mountains. For all of the night nothing moved, and no lights showed as we strolled and talked, and kissed. Then we drove back.

CHAPTER NINE

There had been no letters from James for some time. The absence of letters was almost worse for my parents than the letters themselves. Alone in the house I had the odd feeling that he was not far away, as if his spirit still lingered unhappily around the bookshelves, where my mother had neatly stacked his school notebooks to await his return. I don't know how I sensed this, but often with my brothers I'd know what was going on long before anyone else.

Then one day Peter said:

"I saw your brother the other day. Going up the Shore Road."

"You can't have. He's at Oxford."

"I did. On the Shore Road. I swear to God." I'm not sure about this; there's a lot of weirdness going on, now the army's here. One day I'd been out buying cigarettes, and came across a patrol spread out along the road, walking backwards, with their rifle butts held against their hips, the loaded muzzles following the line of the rooftops. Around them everyone was going about their business. Otherwise it was a good day, with the sun shining again, and the people going in and out of the shops, and chatting as they cleaned their front windows or swept the steps. In the middle of it all there was the army patrol, skipping along from doorway to doorway, watching the rooftops, the cars, and any of the windows with their curtains drawn, or thick nets up.

It's a while after this that we started hearing stories within stories; an ordinary story generally started like this:

"A man was found shot today on the road to Lisburn. He was named as Peter McCloskey. No one has claimed responsibility." It's clear what happened and the man is dead.

But then, maybe not immediately, but a few weeks after, things begin to be heard about Peter McCloskey:

"D'you remember that wee fellow Peter Mc–whatshis-name that was shot the other week out in Lisburn with no explanation?"

"Yes."

"Well, you know they found an army ID on him. He was out of the SAS. In plain clothes, he was. And he's the third one this year!"

"No!"

And then perhaps you'd hear something different:

"Do you remember that wee fellow McCloskey that they blew away the other day?"

"Aye."

"Did you not think it strange at the time that no one was ever convicted?"

"I did."

"D'ye know who paid the defence for the fellows they charged with the murder?"

"I do not."

"Only the military. And not only that, but when the fel-lows they'd charged with it got off, they was driven away in an army Land Rover! What d'you think of that, eh?"

Or even more strangely, the later the stranger:

"Have you had cheap laundry done of late?"

"I have not. It costs an arm and a leg, so I do my own collars."

"Well I'd watch out if you's get offered cheap laundry."

"Why, for God's sake?"

"It's the military. They're taking in cheap laundry and doing analysis on it."

"What kind of analysis?"

"Testing for any whiff of gelignite."

"My laundry for explosives? You must be joking. The only explosions in my laundry are when I've had a plate of beans!"

★

Instead of hearing from James, we had letters from Tom.

" 'We've been out rowing in number three boat,' " read my mother.

" 'It is very exciting. There are twenty of us in a boat, and the tidal run around Anglessey . . .' "

My mother paused. "Anglessey? I'm sure that's not right, now is it, shouldn't it be one 's'?"

"Get on with it!" I said.

" 'The tidal run around Anglessey is very strong. Even with all twenty of us rowing sometimes we cannot make any headway. A lot of the boys here are from Liverpool and have their fathers in the merchant navy. In fact I'm the only one from Ireland at all. The discipline is very strict. They've taught me to darn socks and jumpers. Can you send me some more socks as its very cold early in the morning when we've to go out on parade.' "

"Oh dear, it does sound hard," said mother. "I do hope we've done the right thing for him. But he sounds well, doesn't he Bernard? Listen here at the end he says: 'Can I come down to Kerry with you in the summer? I'd like to sail our boat down there one day.' "

My father sucked his pipe thoughtfully at this. I could tell that somewhere inside his head he was sailing out through the reefs, into the Atlantic surf beyond, with the waves booming on the rocks, with all of us there as we had been. Or maybe he was just thinking discipline for Tom would somehow prevent a repeat of the failures of James. You still never knew with father what he was thinking.

"He can come," he said, vaguely. "Well, let them all come. I mean I can't stop them, can I?" He scratched his head, looking at me speculatively as he did so.

"Just so long as he doesn't end up like his old Dad," he added.

That night, I lay in my bath. The house was unheated, except for the main living room, which had been reduced to a fire at one end when it began to freeze in winter, and the boiler in the dining room on bath nights. With Tom and James away, it had seemed colder still, and emptier. The spaces within the house, the high ceilinged hall and the long landings, now seemed to echo, and the size of the place in no way matched what our needs were at that time. The bathroom, white painted and lino'd, was the coldest room of all. I lay deep down in the hot water, listening to the news on the Home Service on father's radio. The polite voices, so very English, seemed very far away now, mispronouncing every Irish name, misinterpreting every event, as if by sending the army and getting involved they had inadvertently begun to push the island and all of us beyond their understanding. I retuned the radio, looking for music, and heard my brother's voice.

"This is the voice of radio free Belfast, James Grant. Now those of you's who are on the outside of the barricades, these are the opening times for . . ." For a moment I listened, disbelieving. Yet it was unmistakably James.

I jumped from the bath.

"Ma!" I shouted, and ran down the stairs dripping, wrapped in a towel to the living room. "James is on the radio!" She looked up from her reading by the fire.

"Come on! You'll miss him!" I could see she thought I meant the English radio, that perhaps he was being interviewed outside the Oxford Union, or better, had somehow landed a job with the BBC. Together we rushed back up the stairs and into the bathroom, where James's voice continued to outline the arrangements for the Falls Road, and the names of two fellows known to work for the police, who were to be rounded up if they were to be seen, and brought to the Sinn Fein offices.

"Ha! That's brilliant!" I said. "James! For God's sake! Just wait till Tom hears this one."

"But where is he? Where can he be? It's halfway through

term and what on earth is he doing over here?" My mother stared at the radio. Then James gave out a number, which you were to ring if you'd found anyone snooping in behind the barricades, so mother rang and spoke to him and found out that he had come back to Ireland in May, and moved into a flat down behind the University.

Slowly, like a voyage of archaeological discovery, my parents and I traced back what we knew of him, and small fragments began to fall first into a pattern of hypotheses, and the hypotheses to form certainties, as we ate our cereal in the morning, or argued and poured each other tea over supper. We remembered some of the things we'd found in his room; there had been leaflets from the People's Democracy, and the books. There had been no point in him having books on Irish history as he did not need to study this at school. And yet his room was full of them. We remembered the later evenings, and the strange, almost absent presence he had been in the last year before he had gone up to Oxford, and his sudden absences when he had been back in the last vacation. And Tom Riordan and the other lads? We never knew who they were.

The family had an unsuccessful meal with him, which started late, and he came in without apologising, somehow more businesslike in a big green parka, and bustling as if passing through on the way to somewhere else.

"Hiya, Ma," he said, and kissed her cheek perfunctorily, as we did, and nodded at my father, who did not stand up to greet him. And then the questions started, the same questions, circling around the concrete facts of the case, around the fixing of dates, the modes of travel from England to Ireland, the sources of his finances or the lack of them, his every reply seeming to be followed by a sharp intake of breath from mother or a snort from father. But nonetheless the discussion evaded the real issues until my father had pushed away his supper plate, and lit his pipe, and emptied a second bottle of stout into his glass, with his toe tapping away there under the chair, like he was beating out some kind of deadly tune.

"You're a bloody fool you know, James," he began. "You know your history. You know you're wasting your time here. Get on with your life. Get out of here. Get yourself something better. Don't spend any time here. It'll suck you in James, suck you in till you can't get out. Why come creeping back? Go and make your own way in the world. Get out of the womb. Get out of all this bloody tribalism."

"Like you did," said my brother, then he paused. "That's nice coming from you, Da. You just sit there on your arse all day pontificating in your ivory tower. Why don't you do something? Why don't any of you's do anything?"

My father seemed to sink deeper into his chair.

"Like what, James? You can't beat history, James. You know your history. You're the historian around here."

"You can beat history. On the Falls we're beginning to make history, Da! You won't be able to go back. You can't go back. What do you want? Stormont? Back to the old colonial days with the big houses in the country and the poor in their place and the big dinners and the Orange lodge? You're an apologist for your fucking Unionists, that's what you are, Da. By doing nothing, you support them."

"You're wrecking everything," said my father. "You'll pull it all down and there'll be nothing ever to put it all back together again. What are you going to put in its place, James? A United Ireland? Bah! Get back to Oxford and finish your degree. Get some sense."

My mother by now had withdrawn to the kitchen, and crept in to remove the glasses and the plates. When she reached for father's glass, he placed his hand over it.

She tried once to get the conversation going, but I could see it had all been blown away, whatever it was that had kept us civil with each other. Was it my father? Was it James? Whatever was the case, when the evening ended my mother saw James to the door. Outside I could see the rain slanting down in the streetlights as he turned up his collar.

"Let us know how things are," she said. "And if you need anything." Then James turned away into the night, pausing for a second to light a cigarette in the shelter of the porch, inhaling deeply, as if free of all of us.

Back in the house the old man had grabbed the seat by the fire, and had the television on with all the horror stories up on the screen again.

We'd arranged she would come up to Belfast. This time I'd a proper plan and the parents were meant to be out, but in the end father had got cold feet about being invited to dinner and cried off. I'd rung Elaine to try to warn her and to arrange to meet somewhere else, but it was too late.

"She's left already, Patrick," Elaine's mother said.

"I thought you's were going out," I said to mother.

"We were, but Bernard's got a migraine," she said, still dressed as if for dinner, but now with an old cardigan wrapped round her shoulders.

"You've not been out for ages, Ma," I said.

"I know," she said. But father was in his old painting trousers, by himself on the sofa, airily enjoying the throbbing tones of Mahler and I could see there was no moving him. Never mind that, I thought; I would change quickly and intercept Elaine at the bottom of the road before there was any chance of her meeting them.

But she was early, so I was still shaving and trying not to cut myself where the spots were, wincing in the mirror, when the doorbell rang.

"There's a girl here," mother shouted up. When I came down she was in the hall talking with mother, as I did up my trousers and tucked in my shirt.

"Hi, you's," she said. Then the door to the living room opened and father peeked out, then emerged, holding his whisky glass, with the noise of the music booming out behind him.

"Hullo, there!" said Elaine.

"S'my Da," I mumbled. "S'my Ma.

"Hullo," she said, and gave them both a radiant smile. "I'm Elaine."

"So where are you from, Elaine. Patrick's not told us anything about you."

"He's such a dark horse," said father.

"I'm from Markethill. We've a farm," said Elaine. Comprehension dawned on mother.

"Aha," she said. "So that's what all the weekends in the country were about."

"Bandit country," said father.

"Not really," said Elaine. "There's a wee bit of bother an' all." I could see his eyes, as she smiled at him. I had become stuck on the stairs, half dressed. Any minute and they would have her sat down drinking tea.

"I'll be down in a minute," I said desperately.

"Would you like a cup of tea, Elaine?" said mother. Elaine glanced up at me.

"We've to go," I said, decisively. But I could see already they liked her. She lit up the hall, the gloomy, fusty hall where the clock ticked and the black telephone lay silent. I could see them already, latching onto her, sucking something from her, something that I wanted for myself.

"They seem nice," she said, when we were finally in the car.

"Aye. They're alright." I said.

She drove easily, assertively, as if accustomed to going out in the city. The car was filled with her scent again, musky, warm, exotic. A pair of furry dice bounced from the rearview mirror.

"Who's the fellow who's having the party?"

"S'a friend of Tom's. He's his own flat."

"Is it a big party wi' a band?"

I'd no idea. As I'd never had much experience of parties I didn't know.

"Probably will," I said.

"D'yez need to bring a drink?"

"I've me Da's sherry." I said.

"Sherry! We's could stop and get some lager."

I wasn't sure we could. I fingered my money, wondering what lager cost.

Then we came up to a roadblock and Elaine had the window down laughing and joking with the squaddy on the barrier as he peered in the back, and looked straight through me at her as he handed her back her driving licence.

"They're 3 Para," she said, when we'd been waved through. "They've just come."

The party was in a small terraced house down a side street, on the ground floor.

"Tom's invited us," I said. The fellow on the door looked doubtful. "He's away at sea now," I explained. Then Elaine stepped into the light and he waved us through, pressing himself against the wall in the narrow corridor and peering down her cleavage as she passed.

They'd two rooms, one with the record player in playing music that was empty and obviously intended for dancing, and the other for the drinks, which was full of fellows in jeans, with their hair slicked back, smoking and drinking beer by the can.

We stood around, the music stopping from time to time as the party-giver changed it to see if he could provoke some dancing, and I drank down a couple of paper cupfuls of red wine.

"Yez've another brother?" she asked.

"Oh, aye. Old James." I said. "You'll not see him partying. And Tom, who's in the navy." A girl came up then and asked me breathlessly was I Tom's brother. She was heavily made up, her lips the palest I'd ever seen. I basked for a moment in her avid attention, reflected from the absent Tom.

"When's he back? He never told us he was off."

"Don't know," I said, genuinely not knowing.

"Soon?" she asked.

We went through and danced to the 'Beatles' and the 'Stones', the small room sweaty and dark, and the party filled up. Then they put on the slow numbers and Elaine slipped into my arms. I could feel her body, light and strangely soft. When she danced, she seemed to float on air.

"That feller's a dish," she said, looking over my shoulder.

"Give us a break. Everyone's a dish to you," I said.

"Only you," she said.

When we went back out for more drink, there was only sherry left, though I could see some of the hard cases had filled their beakers with it.

"Here, some eejit's brought sherry," said one, chucking it back and grimacing, then filling his paper cup again from the bottle.

We went outside where it was dark. Washing still hung on the line; bachelor underwear, rugger shirts, blowing in the wind. We smoked and chatted.

"My brother's a maniac." I said. "People's democracy. He's a red-hot republican."

"But yez're not Micks?" she said.

"No. But he's a right diehard." At the time it had seemed to make me interesting to tell her, to make me different from the other boys in their party shirts and jeans, drinking down the last of the booze.

I seethed at being taken away with my parents. But my mother said it was an opportunity not to be missed what with the winter rent they'd been offered for the place, and what happy times they'd always had there.

"I'm afraid you'll just have to lump it," father said, from the driving seat. "We can't leave you in Belfast with everything that's going on."

"There's no telling what you'll get up to."

It was a desolate kind of place, set back from the road, just outside the fishing village of Annalong. The bedroom windows were made of old portholes and the roof was held down by iron bars, bolted into the ground to stop it being lifted by the westerly gales. I recognised the place from some old photographs we had of when we'd been there as toddlers; there's one of my father in happier times, with his stomach out, wearing a one-piece female bathing suit, a straw hat, and a rose in his mouth, pirouetting on the beach. The caption he'd written in the photo album read:

"The duke of Plaza-Toro, taking the waters." And there in the background were the three brothers cavorting on the sand, with myself chubby and wrinkled in nappies. But I had no recollection of having been there as we turned in through the gate, and parked the car by the house.

I climbed out, and the winter wind nearly knocked me flat. I could hear it humming and moaning in the iron bars that held the roof down, while father found the keys. I looked about at the view, such as it was, over the grey Irish Sea on the one side, and the flat sodden fields on the other, with the mountains rising beyond. Then father let us in and down a long narrow corridor to the living room.

Once inside the cottage and the door closed against the wind, my father went into the kitchen to fetch an oil lamp and the methylated spirits for lighting it, and started pumping up the pressure in the tank as the dusk settled outside. My mother went out into the scullery and started peeling the spuds. I hung at the windows, hearing the wind riffling through the cracks, and the noise of the winter sea on the stone beach. In the distance, the Mourne Mountains were turning dirty black, the clouds rolling in.

"Jeez, Da, it's cold," I said.

"Light a fire then," he snapped at me.

In the kitchen I found mother had brought the lighters and some wood. She didn't look up from the sink as she peeled potatoes, there in the gloom, with a guttering candle on the ledge above.

Once I'd got the fire going and father had got the lamp lit, he got his patience cards out of their box and mother got out her knitting and I found I couldn't stand it, the two of them settling down for the night at half past four in the evening.

"I'm away for a walk," I said. In a minute or so he'd ask:

"Are you ready for a sherry," meaning "I'm ready for a whiskey," and then I knew they'd pour the drinks and he'd switch on the radio, and listen to the early evening news while she knitted away.

Outside the cottage there was a path which led down a steep bank to a stream and a farm track. I followed the track down to the beach in the dusk. The beach was just old rock and stones stretching away to the end of the bay, and the Irish Sea, cold in the rain, with the waves moaning as the wind ripped the crests off them. I stumbled along the shoreline, the seaweed popping and slipping under my boots, and the rain beginning to come in steadily, across the rock pools. Looking back, I could just see the oil lamp burning in the cottage on the promontory. It was uncomfortable. It was wet. I'd learnt nothing. I knew Elaine might be in Belfast with Peter and his family that weekend. What would they be up to? What would I be missing?

I turned back up the path and walked swiftly, my feet taking me up past the house, not bothering to duck down, and away up towards the main road where I'd seen a phone box. I crossed a big field full of cows, vaulted over an iron gate and stood out on the main Newcastle road, wet with rain. The occasional car went past, the noise of its tyres shushing in the damp. Inside the phone box I dialled hurriedly and Elaine answered.

"Jesus it's you," she said. "I was ringing but got no reply. How're ye keeping? I was wondering if I'd hear."

"What're you up to?" I asked, but before I could get an answer she was on asking about events in the city. I said things weren't bad, or not as bad as it might appear if you listened to the news, and then explained where I was.

"Is there any chance of meeting up, eh? Can you not get down and rescue me?" I asked.

She said that she could and I floated off back down the path to the house, with the rain dripping down my neck. I opened the front door and the corridor to the living room was cold and dark, with the yellow light of the oil lamp showing under the door at the other end. When I stepped into the living room, my parents were just as I had left them; my father had the patience cards out on the table and was turning them over, and my mother was still knitting. The fire had settled. The whisky glass was nearly drained by my father's side, my mother's sherry untouched on the nook by the fire.

"Ah. There he is!" said father, almost relieved.

"Are you not frozen out there?" said mother. "You were out for a long time." And then my father stood up and stretched, and went to the window and peered out through the curtains at the weather.

"That's a dirty night now," he said. The radio was on, giving news of another bomb which'd gone off, but no one commented. I didn't care.

She picked me up the next morning as we'd arranged, from the end of the path. The day was a great deal brighter, and we chatted as the car skimmed along the empty coast road. The high street in Newcastle was empty of shoppers and we stopped for cigarettes and coffee, and I kissed her as we stood waiting for our drink. The coffee was watery and lukewarm and we shared a cake, pulling it apart, our fingertips touching, smiling at each other.

"Jeez, its great to be away," I said.

"Isn't it," she said, her finger running round the edge of the coffee cup, the long nails painted. I could see her knee tapping with just a hint of impatience.

"We'll away to Belfast, will we?" I said.

"There's no one in the house is there?" she asked.

"No," I said. There was a pause, then, and she looked at me, her eyes looking for something, hesitating. She reached her hand across the table and my hand closed on hers.

"Right," she said, standing up. "We'll go there then." And then she picked up her car keys, cigarettes and lighter, and tossed them into her coat pocket.

The house seemed strange without them. The door opened on a few letters, and the previous night's "Belfast Telegraph". The cat appeared from nowhere, roused by our arrival, and stirred around her bare legs as she bent to stroke him.

"Ah, they've not left the cat, have they?" she said. All I could think of was how I'd get her up the three flights of stairs to the bedroom. "He's a lovely cat. What's his name?"

"Boris," I said. "Na. Only joking."

"Ah, fuck off, would you," she said. I closed the door. It was a big heavy door and blocked out the light. The house smelled musty already, I thought, and the curtains had been carefully drawn to save the carpet from fading. She walked around, almost on tiptoe, as if the place were a museum after closing time. She pushed open the door into the living room, then the dining room. As each door opened, light flooded the hallway.

"My room's upstairs," I said. "C'mon and I'll show you."

"Is it indeed?" she said. I was already on the stairs and started to walk up, hoping she would follow.

When I reached the top I heard her voice behind me.

"Steady on," she said.

When I got in the room I found I didn't know what to do, there in the light, cold, airy attic room with the remains of the train set stuffed in the corner, the schoolbooks strewn and all the archaeology of childhood laid out there before her. She stopped, in the middle of the room, and turned around, taking it in.

"So this is where you live?" she said.

"Exist more like," I said, trying to distance myself from eveything there, wishing now I had taken her anywhere else but here. Quickly, I opened up the skylight and the window to let the air in.

She let her hand trail across the dust of my train set, still decaying in the corner, and then over my books from school, the pages of essays, tossing them over.

"What is it you're studyin' again?"

At the time I didn't give a fuck what I was studying. I just wanted her, every part of her; I wanted an end to the messing and for her to be mine.

"A levels," I grunted, and sat on the bed, not knowing where else to go under this gentle scrutiny, this slow exploration.

"And is that okay?" she asked, smiling to herself. "I mean like really, Pat, is that what you want to do?"

"Not at the moment," I said. "Definitely not now."

She seemed to reflect on this for a moment, quite calmly, as if trying out different interpretations of it, her head on one side.

"Well," she said. "What d'yez want?" But before I could even begin to think answering, she raised her arms above her head, showing bare midriff, tossing her hair loose from its grip.

"I was never any good at school," she said suddenly. "Never any fucking good at all. When I left I burnt me books. The whole fucking lot of them, up in the air!" She kicked one leg high in the air, touching her toes as she did so; this slight, innocent, unexpected act mesmerising me.

"Ballet," she said. "Have you seen my ballet?"

"No," I said.

"Well, watch this." Then she raised her hands above her head and stood on tiptoes and pirouetted on her points, elegantly before me.

"Where'd you learn that?"

"Just did it," she said. "It came naturally." She stood, looking at me, and then, nervously, tentatively, held out her hands to me in the cold late morning light of my room, and I stepped forwards and held both her hands.

"D'yez think I'm any good?" she said.

"I do," I said. "I think yez're excellent."

"Of aye," she said, unconvinced, as my hands slid up over her hips, feeling the smooth softness of her midriff and then up under her thin top, her lips kissing me, at first clumsily, then hungrily.

"Do you? Do you think I'm good?" she said again, but this time she'd her hands on my belt and I'd her jumper off and I did not care whether she was good or what or anything.

We plunged under the icy sheets, under the blankets that mother'd piled on the bed for the winter mornings, crammed in together, a struggle of knees and underwear, her hot smooth body pressed in beside me, as she drew me out.

"Ah, fuck Jesus," she said, as she touched me there for the first time, her eyes closed, my hands running over her body at last, over all of her.

"Just hold me for a moment," she said. "And promise me youz'll not be cross with me. Whatever I does?" I pulled back and looked her in the eyes, and she looked back at me and I could see that she meant it, that she wanted me, but was afraid of what she might do to me, and it made me want her more, to find out what that was. And my prick was nuzzling her hot, bare sex.

"I promise," I said, and slid into her soft, yielding body, while the room, the house and all of everything else was forgotten for one first, vital, moment.

Then later I half heard the sound of the car coming up the drive and then my father's weary voice in the garden, like the end of hope, saying:

"I expect he'll be here with that girl."

Elaine was curled up against the cold, under my arm.

"C'mon my folks are back!" I said, trying to get upright.

I heard their key in the lock and my mother calling:

"Patrick," in that high-pitched, penetrating way of hers. But Elaine giggled loudly, the laughter coming up, at first suppressed.

"Patrick!" She mimicked my mother and stifled her laughter as we struggled into our clothes.

CHAPTER TEN

Then James rang again and we had to have him over, as he'd someone to introduce.

"This is Siobhan," he said. My mother was formally polite. "Where are you from, Siobhan?"

"I'm from Derry," she said. "But my folks come from Donegal."

"So, eh, did you go to school in Donegal, Siobhan?"

"St Columb's. In Derry. I never liked it."

Throughout the lunch she talked in a lively, animated way, and smoked, and seemed to me like a pleasant kind of person, but the more she chatted the more my parents became silent.

Then after lunch, the arguments started again. I found my mother taking refuge in the kitchen, as usual.

"Your father gets so cross," she said. "It's because he sees James as so like himself." We could hear him now, into his second bottle of stout.

"And where the bloody hell will that get you?" and my brother arguing back, in a new, loudly confident way he had, a fluent torrent of speech that left no room for words to counter his arguments, even if words could be found to do so, and then Siobhan's voice joining in, shrilly, and the sound of chairs being shoved back and the front door slamming again.

"James's throwing his life away," said mother. "He used to be so clever. He was much the cleverest of all of you, you know." I felt uneasy with this sudden knowledge. I had never known who was top of the class in her book, and now that school was nearly out, here was the final ranking.

"I do wish Bernard wouldn't drink," she added. "He gets so argumentative, you know."

★

Silence descended on the house once more, until Tom came home. He seemed far taller. We'd all expected him to wear his uniform, with the epaulettes that mother had sewn in place. Instead he arrived in a suede jacket. He had grown sideburns, and had his hair with a boyish curl at the front. Barely had he got through the door, than the phone rang and a girl he'd met on the plane was after him. He took the phone, and cradled it behind his ear, rolling himself a cigarette as he talked.

"Deborah!" he said. "Good to hear from you!"

His luggage bulged with peculiar items from the places where the Elder Dempster ships stopped along the way. There was an African face mask, with strange, rigid features.

"It looks like your Mum," said father.

Everyone laughed, including my mother.

Guess what, Tom, I now longed to say. Guess what, I've got a girl. But he got there first:

"Amsterdam, Pats. Amsterdam! Wow! They've got these girls there. Christ! Amazing tits! The first mate got up a whip-around for me in the first port we got to, and . . ." He lowered his voice. "Jesus, Pats, I mean really gorgeous! With these really incredible sort of fishnet knickers and suspenders! Wow!" He leapt off the bed in my room, rubbing his crotch. "And when we got upriver, Christ they've got these big black women in the huts down there that you'd not believe." His eyes seemed to bulge at the memory. "Jesus. I'm incredibly horny!"

He roamed restlessly around my room, coming at length to what was left of my train set.

"And what's all this, Pats? You've not still got this?" He picked one of the engines out of the box, peered at it, then dropped it back.

"Old hat, man, it's old hat."

Then he paused, as if remembering where we had started from; peering through the fence as Slieve Gullion had come out from the city, spewing smoke.

"Have the steamers all gone now, then, eh?" he asked. I said that they had. "Too bad," he said. "That's just too bad. And how's James? How's old Jamesy boy? Mum said he'd been in trouble. He was always crazy, you know. Jesus Christ he could never even tie his own shoelaces."

I explained what James was up to, but he didn't appear to listen. Instead he put one foot up on my chair, as if to check that his own shoelaces were tied, and flicked a speck of dust from a highly polished toe.

"Know how much I'm earning?" he asked.

"I don't know."

"Guess."

"Four pounds a week," I guessed. He grinned broadly.

"Twenty-two pounds," he said. "Fourth Mate's pay."

From seeming empty, the house now seemed too full. Tom thundered up and down the stairs and banged in and out of the front door, it seemed for most of the day and a large part of the night. He was filled with an exceptional energy and drive, as if pursued by some private belief that rest equalled lost opportunity. I'd wake at four in the morning to the smell of frying sausages, or the sounds of the Rolling Stones. My father was driven nearly mad by the noise.

Upstairs, in the attic room adjoining my own, Tom had filled an entire wardrobe with his clothes, newly dry-cleaned and wrapped in cellophane. He would try these on in front of the mirror, or take pot shots at the cats with a Chinese air rifle someone on the ship had given him.

"How long is he staying?" asked father wearily, squinting at the "Irish Times" over breakfast, and coughing into a large white handkerchief. I burned with a sense of outrage. I had done well. I had not wasted genius, and here I was still at school, still eating cornflakes with my father, while my brother who had not done well, appeared to have been rewarded.

"Are you seeing Elaine again?" asked mother. I blushed into my cereal.

"Dunno," I said.

"You haven't seen her since that weekend, have you?"

"Dunno."

Father put down his paper.

"What do you mean you don't know? Sounds like a curious affair to me."

"Do you like her?" My cornflakes congealed. I toyed with the spoon.

"Your mother could fix you up, you know," said father.

"Fix me up?"

"Yes, well, young people . . . The things you get up to," he said vaguely.

"Sex," said Mum. "You need to be careful."

Tom bounced into the room, his face glistening with some powerful aftershave.

"Careful of what?"

"Pat's got a girlfriend," said mother.

"A what? *Pat?*" I nodded.

The news seemed to discomfit him, as if he still saw me as we had always been, together as children.

"What's her name?" asked Tom.

"Elaine."

"Oh well, that's all right then. At least she's a Prod," he said.

"A Prod? You can get some Catholic Elaines too. We' ve an Elaine O'Hanlon at work and you can't get more Catholic than O'Hanlon, now can you?"

"Powers," I said. "Her name's Elaine Powers."

"Well you can't get more Protestant than that," said father.

"Let's see her. Have you got a photo?" asked Tom.

I said I hadn't. Did I need a photograph? Maybe I did need a photograph to prove that I had a girlfriend.

"Any letters? Does she write to you?" Letters as well! I needed letters too.

"You'll meet her," said father. "She's a lovely girl."

113

"You mustn't let it interfere with your studies," said mother, patting my hand.

Then the phone rang.

"That'll be yours, Tom," said mother. Mercifully, the conversation stopped. I could hear Tom's voice in the hall saying, "Well, now look, listen sweetie. I never said Thursday." Mother raised her eyes to the ceiling.

"Poor Tom," she said. "He's having such trouble with the girls."

I read about the Easter Rising, from books the other brother had left behind. In fact the whole family had somehow begun to think of him as the other brother. It was disconcerting to know that he was a few streets away from us, and yet he felt further away than when he had been at Oxford. In conversation, mother would lower her voice when his name was mentioned, and my father could never talk of him without some epithet or other, such as "that great idiot," or "the hopeless case." Yet the brother was always there. I read his books by Tim Pat Coogan and James Connolly. I read and reread the accounts of the Easter Rising:

Late on the Friday evening conditions at the GPO reached crisis point. The heavy thunder of the two eighteen pounders that general Low had ordered brought up merged with the roar of the flames licking at the floors below. The wounded Connolly, Padraig Pearse and O'Rahilly decided to make a last break for the houses adjoining.

In the heated climate of the times, some of the images from these stories seemed compelling and haunting, like a secret history of the heart. I could at last see why, in the streets behind my school, there were kerbstones painted green, white and gold, and tricoloured republican flags.

"Padraig Pearse? Who the fuck's he? Some fenian gobshite, no doubt," said McConochy at school the next day.

I could now barely manage to walk through the gates. I hated every part of my school. I hated the uniform, and had torn the badge from my blazer, and wore an old red scarf that was outside the rules. I tried to grow a moustache. One day after school I walked into the navy recruiting office and picked up all the literature. It was full of pictures of unnaturally clean and handsome young people, launching missiles and driving sleek destroyers over azure seas.

"Ach, they're all poofters in the Navy," said McConochy, when I talked about my plans.

Work began to narrow down towards examinations, and all the talk was of grades and universities with far off names. In the mornings sometimes now I'd wake with anxiety gnawing in my stomach. In the evenings, we'd watch the television. Night after night there were scenes of fighting. The worst was the local news before bedtime. My father called it the late night horror movie.

One night in the midst of this my mother jumped up.

"There he is!" she screamed. "Oh God, there he is. It's James in there!"

We all peered at the shadowy figures caught on film, rolling over a police van.

I took Elaine sailing at the height of summer. There was a quiet breeze which darkened the blue water, with tiny scurries of wind, enough to take us to the pub at the end of the estuary. I rigged the boat, and Elaine climbed in. We drifted down on the tide, past Gull Island and around the marker point where the Lough opened out.

We chatted about this and that, with her lying in the front facing me, with her back resting against the foredeck, the sails tied off so there were no ropes to be held.

"My Ma's fed up," she said. "Nothing to do all day. Just mopes around the house."

"Do your folks get on?" I asked.

"They do and they don't," she said.

"Was your Da brought up in the big house?" I asked her. I'd always been curious how they'd lived.

"No one was," she said. "Except Granny. Granny's the only one who remembers. Granny remembers things even before the border. She used to go to balls in some of the big houses out west, in Mayo. She says she had two maids, for herself. She says all sorts of things. Well," her hand trailed in the water, with a light sort of trickling movement. "I mean, at the end of the day and all that . . ." she paused. "Who gives a flying fuck?" And then she laughed, as if expecting to be caught at any moment by the God of history, striking us all dead.

In the pub it was very dark and cool. A Guinness toucan stood with its yellow beak on the point of drinking upon the formica counter. Elaine tipped its beak down, and it dipped to and fro for twenty minutes or so while we talked.

"Mine's a Pernod and vodka. It's called a 'dead Mick' in the regiment," she said.

"A dead Mick?"

"Yeah. All their drinks have got names like that. They've got this thing they do with advocaat and orange called an Ian Paisley, and there's another called a Gerry Fitt, because its green on the top and yellow on the bottom."

There was a silence.

"Tralaalala," she said, brightly. "Oh Jesus Elaine, you've put your foot in it again. What else have they got?"

When we came out, the afternoon was blurred with drink and slightly cooler. The narrow streets of the town were quiet except for the noise of a steam crane, lifting coal down by the harbour. We climbed down the long ladder from the quayside to where the boat now hung, half full of water, beached by the low tide. The sea was warm around our ankles as we dragged it out, barefoot through the shallows, our feet sinking in the mud.

★

Then, when we got back to Belfast my mother said father needed a lift up from the university, and would Elaine and I mind picking him up?

"Queen's?" said Elaine. "I'd like to see it." So we went to the common room to find him.

"Ah there you are!" he said, stepping from the gloom. The bar was thickly carpeted and discreet, modern before its time, with a lot of stripped pine, fabric wallpaper in subdued colours, and low seating arranged to encourage conversation.

"Let me get you a drink," he said. The staff were attentive, my father more so. When the drinks came, he steered us over to some free seats by the window. The lights were down, even though it was early evening. As he guided us along he nodded, first to one side, then the other, recognising people.

"Jimmy! Annette!" he murmured. Then we settled on the low seats, his eyes wandering to Elaine's legs as she sat down.

"This is a great place," she said.

"Isn't it," he said. "Its new."

"Cheers," he said, draining his glass.

Elaine held her glass carefully, as we talked, sipping her drink from time to time.

"Would you like another?" he said, a minute or so later.

"I'm fine thanks, Mr Grant."

"Ach, come on you could squeeze one in there. Pat? What'll it be?"

"I'll have a Guinness," I said, waving my empty glass at him.

"Sammy!" snapped my father, nodding to the barman to attend to the empty glasses. "We'll have the same again all round."

When I took him home as mother had instructed, he had a bit of a struggle to get his coat on, to manage his umbrella and his briefcase and his hat.

After Elaine had gone I overheard him in the kitchen with mother.

"That Elaine's a lovely girl," he said again. "A lovely girl."

"And so pretty!" said mother.

"I think yer Da fancies me," said Elaine later, tossing her hair, and doing her lipstick, quite unconcerned, maybe even slightly pleased.

And then I noticed him staying out late, with his chops left in the oven to congeal. When he came in my mother would place them on the table for him, shrivelled up. He'd pick at them for a bit, then fall asleep in front of the television, with his head thrown back and his collar undone.

"Yer Da's keen on boats," said Elaine, a few days later.

"Aye," I said, not expecting what was to come.

"Da's a yacht," she said. "Down at Carlingford. He'd take him out."

I considered this. While a day on a yacht was an attraction, a day on a yacht with her father or mine was definitely not, and the two together was to be avoided. I couldn't see them having anything in common, the one burly and bluff, and the other with his head lost in the clouds of god-knows-what. But then again they might get on and my father had a fondness for fellows with a commonsense approach.

But what would it say about the two of us? Why was she asking me? I looked at her lounging there seductively with her long, bare legs stretched out, leaning back against the wall of my room, one strap of her light summer top hanging loose.

"It'd be a laugh," she said. "A gas. Come on! Can you see your Da and mine?"

"Will they not get ideas," I said.

"What do you mean, ideas," she said innocently, pulling me down by the hand, so we could kiss, my lips meeting hers, my tongue seeking hers, my hand slipping under the top.

"Isn't that what ye'd want?" she pulled away for a moment her eyes mischievous. "Sure I thought that was what you wanted," she said, her hands wriggling under my shirt.

"It'd be a laugh. Yez love sailing too," she said. I kissed her again, my hands peeling off her top, while she undid my jeans.

"Ah, Jesus!' she moaned, as my hands closed on her tightly denimmed sex, feeling it thrusting up.

"C'mon. Do it to me ... do it to me quick," she murmured.

When we clambered unsteadily over the side from the dinghy, my mother fought to keep her headscarf on in the wind. Once aboard however, the deck felt solid and stable.

"What kind of a boat is it?" my father asked.

"It's a Dominator II," said Elaine's father. "She's got a 200HP Evinrude, GRP hull with a top whack of forty knots. Elaine tells me you've a boat yourself, Bernard." My father stumbled, and held out his hand to help mother into the cockpit.

"Only a dinghy," he said, apologetically. I was conscious somehow of how our roles were reversed, and that now he was our guest rather than vice versa, and felt a strange, uncharacteristic tang of pity for him, in these unfamiliar surroundings.

We helped Mr Powers throw off the tarpaulins and opened up the hatches, Elaine tripping lightly along the scrubbed wooden deck, the smell of warm new paintwork and varnish mixing with the scent of the sea. On either side of the moorings rose the hills, a mass of yellow gorse, with the sky blue overhead.

I went below with Elaine to get the things for lunch. In the main cabin it was dark and cool with the sounds of water running along the sides, and the reflection of the waves playing on the cabin ceiling. Sweat ran down the back of my neck.

"This is some boat," I said.

"Aye," she said, and then suddenly she was in my arms again, her lips faintly salty. I could hear her father's heavy footsteps, moving to and fro on the deck above.

When we climbed back out, the sunlight blinded me

momentarily. Her father seemed to glance at us, a piercing, angry glance. My head hurt, and my mouth was dry.

Then the engines raced as we prepared for sea, and her father was bellowing something about the fuel lines and how they were reinforced with stainless steel, and the air was full of the smell of petrol. Then I realised what it was that I had seen on the cabin wall down below, in pride of place: the photograph of her father in his uniform, with the high cap, holding his machine gun, with the lads behind him, with their tunic tops, and their working men's trousers, as if they'd not had time nor inclination to change for their photo being taken. They'd all got guns.

When the boat hit the seas it bounced and tossed, sending up showers of spray. Elaine's father held the wheel, while mother clung on in the cockpit, father bracing himself against the cabin roof, while Elaine chatted away, smiling, her hair blowing in the wind.

"So Elaine tells me you've a son at sea," said Mr Powers.

"Oh yes, he's doing very well. Officer training," said mother.

"How many sons have you got?"

"There's just the three," she said. There was a slight pause then, and she added, "the other son's away at Oxford. He's doing very well. He's reading PPE." My father snorted.

The wind hummed in the rigging. In the end I took Elaine up to the bows, away from them, and we found a space to sit, while they talked on. At the bows the air blasted past us, incredibly fresh, making our eyes water. Small pockets of foam flew past. Looking back I could see my mother sitting with her jumper tied around her neck. Later she put it on and called to us were we cold, and wouldn't it be better to go down below and hadn't she wished she'd brought a coat. I could see the Irish Sea all around; the green slide of the waves marching past, the foam sizzling in our wake as we motored on through the afternoon.

My father seemed more at ease when we rejoined them at the stern, smiling and sniffing the air.

"I'm sorry my wife couldn't come," shouted Mr Powers. "Boats make her boke up. Like dolly mixtures! Over the side, eh!" he added cheerfully.

At dusk we turned into the harbour entrance.

"Do you never take her down South?" asked father.

"Never," said Elaine's father. "Never mix with the heathens."

"I see you were in the police, Mr Powers," I said.

"The specials, not the police," he said. "There's a bit of a difference."

"Aye," I said. "I know."

"That's an interesting job," said mother.

"Aye," he said. "And a hard one.

And then he was off reminiscing about the old days when everything was in its proper place as the dusk crept up the estuary and the colour seeped from the hills and the sea.

"That was some gin palace," said my father, as we drove home.

He drove easily, with the window open and his pipe lit, the smell of heather blowing in off the hills as the road twisted and turned back towards Belfast. My mother was silent and thoughtful.

"Are they well off, then?" she asked, at length.

"Aye! Protestant ruling class," I said, mimicking James.

As we came back down into the city we could see all the lights spread out below. I was pleased to be back, that the day was over. But it had not gone well: I'd seen Mr Powers' sideways looks at father; his sharp glances beneath the front he had on. As we'd tied the boat off, and battened everything down on the moorings he'd patted my shoulder in a final kind of way.

"Well, that's that, Pat my son," he said. "Let's get back on dry land."

121

The moorings were washed in a mauve light, with the faint sounds of boatwork drifting: the creak of rowlocks, the chink of glasses and bottles, and the gentle slip-slop of the sea.

"C'mon Elaine, will yez get a move on," he'd snapped at her.

CHAPTER ELEVEN

Peter passed his driving test and to celebrate, we drove down to Markethill together with the radio playing, and smoking all the way. But as we crested the hill and the farmhouse came into view, I saw at once that things had changed.

On the drive was a light armoured vehicle, incongruously parked alongside the family estate car. The rear doors were open, and three soldiers lolled inside, apparently idle. I could see her father washing the car, the hose spilling water out over the path. As we turned through the gate her father paused for a moment, then resumed swabbing with urgent, angry sweeps of his sponge across the bodywork.

We found Elaine and her mother in the kitchen, talking to a young officer. He was not a great deal older than me, clean shaven and tanned. His forearms were muscular, and he spoke with a middle-class Midlands accent that was confident and assured, while Elaine listened.

When we were introduced, he turned and shook my hand, with what seemed a friendly smile, his palms dry and firm.

"Simpson. Captain Simpson."

"Patrick," he said. "That's a damned fine Irish name, isn't it?" But the makings of a frown tugged at the corners of his eyes, a slight, repressed nervousness, as if he was uneasy to have two unfamiliar young men suddenly in the small kitchen. Elaine's mother moved clumsily in the cramped space.

"And how're you boys?" she asked. "How're them exams?"

"That's some vehicle you've got there," said Peter.

"It's a Cheetah," the Captain said, relieved. And then he was off, explaining what it could do and how hard it was to knock out, and then on to how he'd driven them in Oman. I looked at Elaine, dressed as she was in a light summer top, with a thin gold chain at her neck, her eyes large, watching the officer as he spoke and smiling at him, then glancing from time to time at me.

The tea was poured out and her mother filled a plate with biscuits.

"Would you not open a window there Elaine," she said. "And let in some fresh air."

Elaine reached up, showing her smooth stomach and I could see the officers eyes on her. Small gusts of air off the garden stirred the curtains.

Her father came in, carrying the chamois leather and the shampoo he'd used for washing the car. He nodded at me.

"I see that brother of yours is in the papers again," he said shortly. I was hemmed in against the wall, by the kitchen table. I suddenly wished I'd not mentioned James or any of his doings, to Elaine. At the time it had seemed funny, unusual. I thought it had made me interesting, having a brother on the other side. I thought my mother had kept it secret too.

"Is he?" I said foolishly, trying to think.

"Civil rights!" he snorted. "If they can't be civil, they shouldna' have rights!"

Elaine's mother poured out the tea. Elaine began to brush out her hair, mesmerised into indifference by the first mention of politics.

"Yes," I said.

Her father's shirt was open at the neck, with ginger hairs curling out of it. He'd a large face, "A protestant face," my father would now say, as if faces could be named, and ranked, in that way.

"Yes, what?" he said, half teasing, but only half. "I hope you's have none of your brother's ideas."

"Ach c'mon, leave him alone," said Elaine's mother.

"He's nuts," I said. "The brother is."

The officer leant forward in his chair, listening keenly, wiping the crumbs from the biscuits off his combat trousers.

"Sinn Feiner is he, then?" he asked. "Your brother."

"Na. He's nuts," I said again, feeling disloyal as I said it.

"Well, he's in the right country for that," said the Captain, standing up and stretching, showing the dark patches of sweat under the armpits of his heavy combat tunic, and everyone laughed.

"You're right there, Captain. You certainly are!" said Mr Powers.

"I must be off," said the Captain. "The men'll think I'm up to something if I stay too long."

"Will you not have some more tea? We'd be glad for the company," asked Elaine's mother. He smiled again, and glanced at his watch.

"No, really, I'd love to, but . . .

"Duty calls . . ." Mr Powers completed his sentence and saw him to the door, holding his elbow in a friendly sort of way.

"Come on you lazy fuckers!" He shouted at the men. Elaine giggled. Silence fell in the kitchen before it was drowned by the noise of the motor on the armoured car firing up, killing all hope of conversation, making the windows rattle, filling the driveway with blue diesel fumes, which drifted in through the kitchen window.

Later, Peter went off to say hullo to his grandparents and I went up to Elaine's room.

"So, who's the fellow with the tank?" I asked.

"Oh, the Captain," she said. "He's a tosser." The word, an English word, did not sound right as she said it. I wondered where she'd learnt it from.

"Is he up here a lot?"

"They're on patrol, from Armagh," she said. "It's boring. I suppose that's why they come over."

We lay on her bed for hours, watching the clouds as they drifted by behind the picture windows and the light changing on the fields and bracken on the hills towards the border. She put on her record player, and we danced, barefoot in the small, stuffy bedroom.

"Mum wants me to get a job," she said. "I'd like to be a model, or something." She paused, looking at herself in the mirror. "I could be, except my mouth's too large. What d'you think?"

She could have been anything, I thought, as no one could refuse her.

I went with her to see "Curse of the Thing" in Armagh the following week. Her hair was unbrushed and she gave non-committal answers to all my questions as we parked up outside the security barriers and walked down the main street in the rain. There was a good crowd for the film though and in the bright lights of the foyer everything seemed almost normal, with the boys and girls smartly dressed, buying popcorn, and an air of reasonable humour all around. As we queued, I could see some of the fellows peering at her, like they did, wherever we went.

"What've you been doing?" I asked.

"Ah, this and that," she said. "And yourself? What have you been up to Patrick?" She wasn't looking at me. In the film, I tried to hold her hand.

"I'll drop you back to the station," she said, when the film was over.

"What's wrong?" I asked.

"Nothing," she said. "It's just nothing." I tried to pull her towards me, to pull her hair back from her face to see her expression, but she pulled away from me into a pool of darkness.

"It's nothing. Just leave it will you?"

"OK."

When she swung the car into the station the train was already in, and we hadn't much time.

"Come and see me again," she said, leaning from the window. "You promise?"

126

At school I tried to get what it was out of Peter, but he just grunted and said he didn't know, which made things worse. I remembered her telling me how thick they were; how they'd as good as been brought up together.

"Peter'd do anything I say," she'd said.

School had started early that year. There were elections for the assembly at the time and one of our teachers had thought it a grand idea that Ulster's teenage boys should have a chance to debate the vital issues of the day by organising a mock election in the school.

McConochy swaggered round the long, straight corridors, bouncing from wall to wall as he went, canvassing in his own particular way.

"Unionist, or you're head's kicked in!" or "Grant! See you! I've got your fucking number!"

There was a wee fellow in our class at the time, called Cyril who had a way of taking the contrary position on almost anything you cared to mention and who was about ten times cleverer than any of us, always rabbiting away in answer to the teacher's questions with a load of brilliant stuff no one had ever heard of or could understand.

A few weeks before the election Cyril surprised us all by starting to slap up posters on the walls, the like of which you'd never seen in a good Protestant school, posters for the other side. Of course they weren't there for long, as the head had his janitors out ripping them down, scrunching them up and putting them in the bin, that is if McConochy hadn't got there first writing, "Taig" and, "F.T.P" in felt tip all over them. But Cyril had the posters back out again and posted up on the windows and doors as quickly as they were ripped down. I was helping him. I didn't like the place, with its bare floorboards, bare walls, and ancient desks all carved to bits with initials. The school had high Georgian windows, and cold wintry light filled it, even in summer. I didn't like McConochy and remembered how he'd treated me when I started at the school. Anything that caused bother for the school, and for McConochy, was alright by me. So me and Cyril slapped our posters back up again, sellotaping them on tight, all round the edges.

Then the next day we found big Union Jacks breaking out everywhere, on top of our posters, and the head warned us all in assembly, by which time the poor teacher who'd had the bright idea in the first place was looking a bit embarrassed, what with all the other teachers whispering away and grinning behind their hands that anyone could have been so stupid as to try having a mock election in the current climate.

The Union Jacks however seemed to stay up. We even found Union Jacks stuffed in our lunchboxes, and in our school-bags. There was a real plague of Union Jacks, wherever you looked, until Cyril went up to McConochy and said to him one lunch hour:

"Did you put a Union Jack in my lunchbox?" McConochy just smirked. "I don't want your Union Jack in my lunchbox," said Cyril, and then gave McConochy what was left of the crumpled paper flag. McConochy looked at him like he was some kind of lower animal and looked at what was left of the flag.

"I've a right to fly the flag of my country anywhere," he said. "Anywhere I fucking choose, Cyril, and no one's going to stop me."

By this time there was a big crowd of lads all round, who could sniff a fight before it started, and soon they were all chanting:

"Fight, fight, fight!" and demanding action.

Now Cyril was not the biggest of lads, indeed the idea of Cyril fighting anyone was ridiculous, and some of us could see this. Even McConochy saw this, so he just stuffed the Union Jack into the breast pocket of Cyril's blazer. Cyril stood quite still.

"Like a hanky," he said, looking at the Union Jack sticking out of his pocket. "Like a hanky you could blow your nose on."

McConochy just went bright red. It was like blood rushing up his neck and you could see all the acne, inflamed by it.

"What did you just say?" he said, and gripped Cyril's tie. "What did you just say?"

Cyril stiffened a bit, and McConochy just shoved him back, letting him fall over, clumsily, in amongst the desks, and everyone cheered and shouted:

"Go on. Do him, Mac!" but McConochy just shrugged his shoulders, pulled down his cuffs, and walked off.

After that I took to sneaking off out of school with Peter and sometimes Cyril too. The whole place was fenced in with barbed wire and big steel railings, and there was only one or two places that anyone could ever get in or out of once the doors closed behind you. The best way was to wait till you'd a class in the east block. At the corner where the gate was, you could mingle with the big crowd of lads as they changed classes, duck out through the gate and away down behind the parked cars out into College Square, ripping off your school tie as you went.

We'd do this more and more as time went on, Peter and I. Sometimes we'd go up to the central library and pretend to read, hidden behind atlases and dictionaries, eyeing the girls in their uniforms from the other schools, up to much the same as us, and scheming to get introductions. Then we found out we could get served in the bars.

"What are we going to do, Peter?" I said, when the library had begun to bore.

"We'll away to the Washington, shall we?" he said.

At lunchtimes in the Washington Bar things were quiet. There was cool mosaic stone on the floor, pockmarked here and there, and dark, varnished wood in the snugs where you could hide and talk. The voices of other drinkers murmured as in a church, while the old reprobates who lived in there leant on their elbows, studying the racing pages, on their stools at the high marble bar.

We found a snug, and the waiter, a lad our age, came and served us Guinness.

"Will you be seeing her again?" asked Peter.

"Elaine?" I said.

"Aye, Elaine."

I feigned indifference. I could no longer see where we stood.

"She's been seeing the Captain," he said, watching me.

"Ah fuck," I said.

"You needed to know.'

"I met him." I said. "I could see. He was a wanker."

Peter reflected on this, licking the beer froth from his lips.

"She'll come to a sticky end one day," he said admiringly.

"Aye," I said. "We'll have another, shall we?"

Her father came out of the yard to pick me up, driving the new tractor like a racing car. I'd promised to help with the last of the late harvest as a method of getting back to Markethill. Maybe at the time I'd still fantasies of lovemaking in the hot cornfields, of picking blue cornflowers and tying them in her hair while bare-chested labourers brought in a bumper harvest in the fields below.

"Yer not wearing that?" he said as he drew up to where I was standing on the steps, the tractor coughing as he dropped it into neutral, his forearms vibrating to the revving engine. He was wearing a pair of tan boots and some stout socks and I could see the straw stuck in the wool of them and his bare legs were scratched underneath the ginger hair. His legs were like tree trunks and his chest beneath the shirt was mahogany red.

"Yez'll get ripped tae fuck in that gear," he said, looking at my cotton trousers and my thin Hawaiian beach shirt. I hesitated.

"The lads are halfway over the long field already," he said. I couldn't see where to get up on the tractor. At the back he'd lifted the rakes and the prongs pointed outwards like an array of knives, rotating gently.

"Git up here," he said, pointing to a ledge by his feet, and even before I was halfway up he'd whacked the tractor into forward motion and we launched up the path and away from the barns, with me grabbing at his shoulder for balance.

"Hat?" he shouted. "Have yez got a hat?"

I shouted that I hadn't, the exhaust from the tractor clattering away up in front. He pulled off his own hat and thrust it at me. The sweatband was dark and the hat felt cold and moist to the touch.

"Na. Keep it. Yez'll need it," I shouted. But he ignored me. Halfway down the long sloping path to the gatehouse he turned suddenly sharp right, almost chucking me off, and the tractor dived down a steep narrow lane, unsurfaced and deeply gouged with ruts of mud, the wheels slipping from side to side as we went. Then we lunged through an open gate out onto a broad shoulder of open meadow, high above the surrounding countryside.

As the tractor came to a standstill I could see the whole spread of the estate laid out before me. We were surprisingly high up, on the side of a fertile slope laid to grass and dotted with old trees. A hundred or so cattle grazed there on the luscious green grass. At the bottom of the valley, a stream divided the land from a substantial wood which rose on the opposite side to the long wall which bounded the estate, visible in the middle distance. Further up, at the head of the valley, I could see the cornfield with two harvesters working across it, followed by a gang of men, loading bales.

He switched the engine off and took a bottle out from under his seat, taking a long draw on it before wiping it on his bare arm and passing it to me.

I took a drink and the warm stout boiled and frothed in my mouth.

"Listen tae that," he said.

I listened, but could hear nothing, only the sound of bird-song and the faint whisper of the wind in the hedgerows, and distantly, the revving of one of the combines as it turned at the edge of the long field above. He gripped my arm tightly.

"Listen," he said again. And this time I heard it faintly; the sound of drumming, awesomely, across the fields.

"The boys," he said, beaming.

"Is all this yours?" I asked.

"Aye. Long may it rest." He said, and stowed the bottle, slammed the gears and we descended the field at an angle to cut through another gate into the cornfield below.

"Thirty poun' an hour," shouted Mr Powers as we caught up with the first harvester. "Thirty poun' an hour this lot's costing."

I joined the baling gang for the day. There were four of us in the gang, bent double and coughing in the fine dust coming back from the baler. It was desperate work, as the field had a heavy slope on it, and once the corn was cut the ground became a lumpy mess of stubble and baked clay. He drove his tractor up beside me.

"There," he shouted down. "How'd ye like the country life now?" with his boot revving on the pedal before he was away over to the other machine at the far end of the field and I could hear his voice again, bellowing in the distance.

By midafternoon I'd lost sight of whether we were on the down slope or the up, the sunlight burning our faces, insects erupting from the felled corn, ears of corn down our necks and in our hair. I wondered when he would call a halt. But the gang worked on methodically.

At around four, Elaine and her sister came down with the tea in a couple of big Thermos flasks. By then I'd had enough. Looking up I could see their two horses, picking their way over the rough ground carefully, and the two women, bolt upright, the reins held out to keep their balance on the steep incline.

She looked down at me off her horse and leant over to her sister, smiling and said something to her. Her sister smiled. I could see the men's eyes on her. Then she jumped down and came up to me, fresh, her hair neatly tied back under a headscarf.

"How'dye like the country air then?" she asked. "Hiya Michael, Sean," she nodded at the men. "Liam. How's about ye's?" while her sister poured out the tea to the men, us all standing round, the horses stamping in the heat, their bits slathered.

"Ten minutes," said Mr Powers.

With the machines switched off, an awkward silence seemed to fall on the men, the silence of tiredness. We sipped our tea and stood looking down the valley.

"Had enough?" said Mr Powers.

"Aye," I said.

Back in the house they'd all the windows wide open against the heat, but still it seemed oppressive.

"Whad'ye want to volunteer for that crack for," said Elaine, her legs stretched out across two chairs.

"See how the other half lives," I said. The beer she'd given me seemed to blast straight up my nose into my brain. Her sister flicked idly through a catalogue, occasionally chasing a bug away from her face.

"See they've got them skirts in mauve," she said.

Elaine got up, suddenly animated.

"Jeez, they're gorgeous," she said.

"How much is they?"

"Four poun'"

The silence fell again. I'd finished my beer. I could still feel my heartbeat pounding in my ears.

"I'll wash up," I said, and went out to the bathroom, where

I took my shirt off and my trousers and stood under the shower, the water so cold it stung me, and ran some water from the tap round my mouth. It was then I heard the armoured car come up the drive.

"Elaine," called a voice. "Elaine. It's me."

Somewhere a door slammed, as if someone was trying to block out the noise. Slowly, I put on my shirt and my trousers, but they were torn and stained with sweat. I dried my hair on the towel. I looked at myself in the mirror, and my face stared back, the eyes dark, my face burnt beetroot. I'd a cut over one eye. I looked no different from the fellows in the field.

When I went into the kitchen he was there again.

"Well hullo," he said, again open and cheery, and he shook my hand.

"Just thought I'd drop in." But this time, the sergeant was there in the kitchen too, a big, bullish sort of fellow, with tattoos down his arms, workmanlike, with a cup of tea out on the counter in front of him that Elaine's sister had made for him. When she turned to get the milk for him, his eyes roamed over her behind, where it bulged from her cut-down denims.

"Yes, thank you, I don't mind if I do have a biscuit," he said.

"Or some cake," said the Captain.

"What're ye doing here?" I asked.

"Peacekeeping, aren't we sergeant?" said the Captain.

"The other day they found an arms dump off the road, bang up against the estate wall," said Elaine quickly.

"Two rifles and a thousand rounds," said her sister.

"Da sees lights in the woods at night. You's never know what's goin' on, do yez?"

In the end I asked her to walk with me to the gate.

"Are you's doing a line with these boys?" I asked her. I was furious. I grabbed her hand and twisted it behind her back.

"Don't," she said.

★

134

Whenever I got the chance, I'd ring her. I was desperate. When she spoke, she seemed very far away. Every date I suggested was impossible for her. This was the worst things could be, I thought.

Then I began to find myself round at the other brother's place more and more. Siobhan was always welcoming, despite the chaos the place seemed to be in. There would always be a cup of tea and a copy of the day's newspaper and time for some chat.

"And how's your Da?" I said he was fine, as you do, and she looked thoughtful and said nothing.

"He's a weird one," she said.

"What do you mean, weird."

"What does he do all day? I mean he's loads of time on his hands, hasn't he?"

Truth to tell, I hadn't really thought about this, I said.

"I hear tell he's not seen round the university much," said Siobhan.

"Sure it's still the long vacation," I said.

Then the other brother came in with a cigarette stuck to his lower lip and his shirt-tail out, never having been one for smartness.

"Hiyah Pats. How're ye doing?"

"Aye alright, James," I said.

"Has Liam been in yet with the stuff for Derry?" he asked Siobhan, interrupting our conversation.

"Na," she said, then continued chatting to me, changing the subject.

"And your Ma was telling me you've a new girlfriend. Says she's gorgeous to look at."

"Oh aye," I said.

"What's her name?"

"Elaine. But I'm not seein' her now.

When I'd said it, I felt worse, choked up. Something in my tone drew her attention to it.

"Ah dear." She said sympathetically. "That's love!"

James had some big cardboard packing cases up on the table by then, and had shoved the plates to one side, all congealing eggs and bacon.

"Would you's give us a hand Pats," he said. "I've some stuff to pack up." So I went down the stairs with him and helped him lift some stuff out of the cellar and put it in the cardboard boxes and tape the ends down with parcel tape, so no one could see what was inside. When we'd done a good few boxes, we paused, and he asked whether I'd got the car.

"Aye," I said. It wasn't a big thing, I thought, and after all how else would the other brother get the stuff down to the red star office at Great Victoria Street? And anyway, what was I going to do otherwise, with the empty days now that everything was going wrong?

CHAPTER TWELVE

Then they'd a big dance at the school and bussed in girls from all the Protestant grammar schools to dance till ten in the new hall. They'd laid out the tables with crisps and Coca-Cola, and all the masters and their wives were instructed to come. It was a major event, with a proper band up on stage and big fellows with bow ties and tattoos on the door to weed out anyone who looked incapable with drink. They left all the lights full on, and at about half nine the head teacher intervened to stop any kissing that might have broken out.

"Here," he said, pulling the couples apart. "Treat the lady with respect, boys! You're not down the backstreets now!" It was a miserable night, with the girls as sick as we were, and about the only excitement was seeing the masters and their wives, dressed as human beings, and the incident with the kissing.

"Sure there's no point in them school does," said Peter the next night as we lay around smoking in my room. "A load of old Proddie dogs, and the masters keeping an eye on you." He paused, and slurped back some of the home-brew that we'd taken to making under the rafters. "We've got to get some girls," he said.

"I hear there's dances at the university," I suggested. "There's all sorts go there."

"Na, there'll be more fellows than girls. There always is. And we don't stand a chance, being still at school." He paced about the room at this thought. "Ah Jesus," he said. "Who'd look at us?"

"We could get Elaine up. It'd take her an hour or so. Just for company," I suggested. What could be done? I couldn't get her on the phone, when I plucked up the courage to ring. I was lying awake, dreaming of what we would do, when we did meet, if ever we could.

Peter stopped pacing. Then he said that it was too late, she was too far away, and anyway she'd not be let out as she'd got fellows chasing her like she was a cat on heat.

"Let's go anyways," I said, standing up. "Let's just go to a dance." I had to get out and do something. I felt like my head would explode if I didn't.

"I've the money," I said.

"We've not got the car," said Peter.

"Ah fuck, Peter, we'll walk."

Outside the students' union there was a big crowd of lads and girls all trying to get in. I could see McConochy and some of the boys from the school, in bell-bottom trousers and flowery shirts, and heard the sound of the music.

"Let's away and have a wee drink first," I suggested.

"Will they still let us in?"

"Oh aye. It goes on all night," I said. "Into the wee small hours." Though I hadn't a clue how long it went on for. So we set off to find a bar to get some courage.

Away from the mob at the university, everything was hushed and sombre, with not a thing stirring. There were streets of cars, all parked, and none on the road driving. The streetlights were on, burning brightly, but there was no one there who needed them, only us. It was as if everyone had gone to bed, or gone away, back into the daylight hours. Our feet echoed on the paving stones, so we felt tempted to tiptoe, but when we tiptoed we felt afraid, so we talked loudly, animatedly, until we reached the bar and tapped at the door, and the fellow behind peered out at us and saw we were only schoolkids and not some madman with a bomb in his bag, and let us in.

When we were let into the bar we hit a wall of noise which was all the more remarkable for the contrast with the silence on the street outside. Inside, we saw where everyone had gone. The entire city seemed to have been crammed in the one pub!

And the pub had stretched at the seams, to take everyone in. They'd opened up the backroom and the function room, and the courtyard by the toilets, and the storeroom and the basement and half the landlord's living room, and all the stairs. They'd set up a couple of taps so you could get the drink in any one of the rooms.

There was no point having television or games because everyone was so cram packed in and bursting to let their hair down, the last thing they wanted was bar billiards or darts. And with the crowd and everyone talking we needed to shout to make ourselves heard, which made the noise even more, and with the cram it got hard getting at the bar. We fought our way upstairs to where the crush was marginally less severe, and got ourselves two pints each after queueing for the first, so's we'd not have to go back, and of course getting two meant the queues got longer so some of the lads would just buy three at once and drink one down while waiting for the other two. Then we found a ledge to perch the drink on, and shouted at each other.

"This is brill!"

"Fantastic!"

"Excellent!"

And everyone was letting rip. We knocked back the two beers we'd got, and got another two and forgot all about the dance till eleven or so, when it was time to go. We pushed down the stairs from the first floor, past a big group of men going up, all barging and jolly, with their women in tow, teasing and bickering, and back out into the miserable street where it was even emptier and blacker and more desperate than it was before, though now there was the occasional car going through the red lights, packed with fellows on their way home, or a black cab, doing the territory.

"Jesus!" shouted Peter at the night. "Bejasus. I'm horny to fuck," and had his words echoed back from the tall Georgian buildings.

And then we walked in the middle of the road, down the white line, luminous in the dark. I barked like a dog. We got up the steps to the dance. The steps were full of characters like ourselves. There wasn't a single girl left outside at all. At the door, we stood up straight and grinned and mumbled the school's name, and they let us in, and then we were away up the stairs, with the carpet sticky under our feet and full of couples snogging and fellows being sick and helping each other along to the toilets, and girls plotting in big groups. Then it was onto the dance floor, which was wide and bright and full of lights flashing, and they were playing the latest number.

"C'mon," I said, walking over to a likely girl.

"Would you like to dance?" I said.

"Wha?" she said.

"Would you like to . . ." and I mimed dancing, jigging about a bit.

"Wha?"

"Dance," I said.

"Na." she said. "I'm dancing with my friend."

"What did she say?" asked Peter.

"Says 'not now'." But he did not hear because he was ogling some blonde woman with a skirt up round her waist. He marched towards her, with his arms outstretched.

"C'mon give us a kiss," I heard him say.

"You stupid arsehole." I grabbed his arm and hissed in his ear.

"Look, here's how you do it." I shoved him aside, fired up with the Guinness, and turned towards her to say my, "Do you want to dance?" line again. She shrugged, as if to say, "I don't give a fuck whether I do or not, pal," and turned towards me, starting to shuffle about a bit. I leant over to her ear and asked her:

"What school do you go to?" except that Peter had somehow slipped up beside me, and was jerking around like in some cruel parody of my own movements, with a foolish smile on his face. The girl leant forwards to hear and her hair brushed my cheek, her hand touched my arm. I could smell her scent.

"Saint Dominic's. And you? Are you's at the uni?"

"Na," I said. Her face was heavy with powder in the light. "I'm at Inst."

"Inst," she said, and dropped her arm, "Oh aye."

"Do you know it?"

"Oh aye."

Peter tugged at my arm, mouthing something, like a fish.

"They're all Micks," he hissed.

When the dance ended, they played the national anthem with all the lights full on. There was a room full of us, all slobbering drunk and sweaty, quietly queueing to get out, while the loudspeakers boomed out, "God Save the Queen."

"Surely its not over?" said Peter.

"Where's that girl?", I said. But somehow she had gone, swallowed by the crush.

Out in the street it was momentarily busy, with small groups of people zigzagging across the road, laughing and shouting. Then the crowds vanished and the street was empty again and we set off back up the road.

"I heard a very good joke about a man with two cocks," said Peter, apropos of nothing in particular, as we weaved up the empty street, occasionally rasping drunkenly against the privet hedges along the way.

"One cock was Catholic, the other Protestant." Despite my mood, I grinned at this opener.

"Only I've forgotten the rest." He frowned, as if trying to recall the precise details of the story.

"What religion was the man?" I asked.

"Shut up!" He commanded, then continued haltingly, as if he were filling in the gaps of an ill-remembered gag, as we walked along.

"Well the fellow had the hots for a nun," he said.

"How would that work anyway, having two cocks?" I asked, now inspired by the notion and anxious to help in any way I could. Peter waved his hands for silence, his mouth being momentarily occupied with the neck of a bottle of stout which he'd produced from the depths of his greatcoat.

"He fills the nun with altar wine and takes her up the belfry," he continued. "'By Christ,' says the Nun, 'I am doubly blessed,' as she catches sight of his twin appliances."

Peter paused, his brow furrowed with the effort of explanation. "For the sake of clarity let's call the Protestant cock Ian and the Catholic cock Sean," he continued at length, in a somewhat didactic tone.

"Ah, for fuck's sake Peter," I complained.

"Now unfortunately Ian has grown indecently large at the prospect of deflowering a papist virgin. And this is the most gorgeous nun imaginable!" cried Peter. "Mouthwatering . . . a mouthwatering nun! With black stockings and a tight little pair of pants, high heels, and the most delicious tits, large, but firm with it, the nipples dark and exciting," he says, grinning lasciviously in the darkness.

"Soon enough Ian is making his way towards the tunnel of love. But . . . Sean is not far behind, for while the act of penetrating a nun is forbidden, preventing a Protestant committing mortal sin with one may be seen as a decent Catholic pleasure."

"This is getting theological!" I protested.

"So," says Peter dramatically. "It is a race to the finish. The nun rips off her knickers, revealing the most fantastic fanny either dick has ever seen, and the two dicks start to argue. There's this huge corkscrew-like object composed of the fighting dicks, Sean and Ian," said Peter, floundering insanely now.

"Fuck off Peter, this is ridiculous," I shouted at him angrily, pushing him into a hedge, as his voice rose in a last desperate attempt to complete his joke. With a crash, Peter disappeared from view through the hedge, his voice continuing from the other side:

"But with the fight both become more aroused than ever; Ian by fighting the menace of papacy, Sean by fighting to protect the Catholic church, until with a dreadful scream, both dicks are wrenched from their mountings, clean off! And your man's left with no dick and the nun still panting for it!"

There was a long silence after this. I peered over into the garden.

"Are yez alright, Peter?" I said, hauling him out of it and brushing him down.

"Anyway," I asked. "What about your man? Did he have no say in it? Was he not able to stop the fighting dicks?"

"Certainly not! Sure a dick's got a mind of its own regardless of what religion it is," said Peter.

When we reached home it was nearly four in the morning, so I made him a coffee and sent him stumbling away into the night. As I turned to lock up however, I saw someone else in the street outside, a pale face with its coat pulled up round the collar, and an old felt cap. I peered off the step, but the face was turned away, and whoever it was walked past briskly, and crossed to the far side of the road and away.

I went to bed, and tried to get some sleep, but my mind boiled with images of Elaine, and cruel speculations. Then, as I began to doze off, I heard the unmistakable faint sounds of the key in the front door downstairs, and my father climbing the stairs with a clumsy, surreptitious step.

CHAPTER THIRTEEN

In Tom's absence mother continued to field telephone calls from his distressed admirers, and the postcards and letters came, this time from Scandinavia: Bergen, Tromso, Archangel.

"He'll need to keep his trousers buttoned in Archangel!" chuckled father.

Then one day in late November the phone rang and mother answered:

"I hope you're keeping well wrapped up!" We heard her say.

Tom was in Oslo, and on his way home. Mother yelled down the phone at him.

"That's great. You'll be home for Christmas," she said.

"I suppose we'd better invite him over," said father wearily, meaning James. "We can have a family Christmas," he said, as if it was the very worst thing in the world. And indeed Christmas now had ample components of everything he disliked: tradition and ritual, sentiment and nostalgia, and collective rather than individual endeavour.

"I don't like the food; I hate Christmas pudding, turkey is overrated and the television is appalling," he declared, as he laid in his order of drink for the holiday.

"We don't need all that," said mother.

"Yes I do," he said, decisively.

A few days before Christmas, I found her in the kitchen, deep in preparations.

"I do hope there won't be arguments again. I do so hate them, you know," she said suddenly.

"It's the explaining I find so hard," she added. My mother never seemed to find things hard. It frightened me that she might find things hard. It seemed the same kind of Christmas as it had always been; the kitchen was fully stocked: there was a huge and corpulent turkey, a Fermanagh turkey according to the butcher, "As if Fermanagh has better turkeys than anywhere else!" snorted my father. There were sprouts and parsnips, nuts, carrots, chestnuts, biscuits, cake, tangerines, two kinds of date, three boxes of shortbread biscuits, "From grateful customers no doubt," said father, and all of what he loudly called, "That great, steaming gutbucket that is Christmas." That year I also understood for the first time why our Christmas was like this; that really, she had made it especially lavish to annoy him, because he was driving her mad.

"I do wish he wouldn't drink so," she said, ladling more steamed chestnuts into the mixing bowl. The windows were misted up, the grass outside dank and green. In went the brown sugar, and the turkey stock, the olive oil and the other secret ingredients, and she pounded the mixture with a large wooden spoon.

"And how can I say what James is doing? Tom and you are fine, aren't you, but poor dear James! Oh dear, oh lord his life is in such a mess! I mean what on earth can I say to Mrs Crawshaw? You know her husband was shot dead in '56?"

"Our Mrs Crawshaw next door?"

"We never told you. You were only little. Shot by the IRA in the Armagh campaign. They were all in uniform at the funeral, with a police band lined up in the street. It was just after I'd arrived from England." She went back to beating the stuffing with the wooden spoon, not looking at me, as if seeing the men in her mind's eye.

"There," she said, putting the bowl to one side. "I mean how can you tell Mrs Crawshaw what James is up to, when she asks? You just can't, can you?"

On Christmas Eve I drove round to pick up the other brother and Siobhan from their flat. It was dark, and the pavements gleamed wet in the pale moonlight. When I rang on the bell there were no lights showing. Eventually a curtain was pulled back, and steps came down the uncarpeted stairs to the door.

"Who's it?" shouted Siobhan's voice.

"S'me. Pat."

And then she unlocked the door, and pulled back the bolts, her face a blur in the dark hall.

Inside the flat, in the living room, a fire sputtered in the grate, damped down with slack and smoking. Unwashed dishes lay on the table amongst a clutter of papers, covered with his writing.

"Hiya Pats. How're ye doin'?" said James amiably. "D'ye want a cup of tea?"

"No. We've to get back," I said. "They've everything ready for us." He sighed and hunted for his shoes, while I looked about the place. A big cupboard had been pushed up against the window, and the heavy velvet curtains were pulled over behind that.

"There's been a spate of ladder murders," said Siobhan.

"Ladder murders?" I said.

"It's desperate!" she said. "There was a wee fellow just out of school shot in his bed the other day. The bastards climbed up by a ladder and shot the poor wee boy dead in his bed through the window."

"People round here won't open their doors," said James.

The small room seemed suddenly claustrophobic, the heavy velvet curtains sinister with potential.

"C'mon," I said. "Let's not hang about." We went down the stairs. On the step outside, he hesitated and glanced very quickly up and down the street, not checking the traffic before crossing the road, but checking the hedgerows, the parked cars, the windows and the street corners. As we walked to the car, a patrol passed and he turned his face down into his collar and looked away.

★

"Well now, come on. Come on in both of you!" said mother. "Let me take your coat. We've a fire both ends of the living room, and Tom's due back any minute." She looked at her watch distractedly. "Any minute," she repeated.

Father appeared at the door to the living room.

"Come on," he said, dully. "Come on and have a drink." And then they were ushered into the living room and Siobhan seated herself in father's chair by the fire, and I could see she'd got herself specially dressed up for it, and James was doing his best, as you do at Christmas.

"Well, father, are you still doing your painting?" he asked.

The old fellow seemed not to know where to put himself, what with his chair occupied, so he stood with his back to the fire.

"I've stopped all that long ago," he said, in a lordly sort of way as if it were all beneath him, and he'd now seen some brighter light. Then he became apologetic.

"Ach, I can't seem to get it right," he said. Whatever rightness was, it was true; his painting, like everything he tried, had succumbed to his own dissatisfaction with himself. The paintings had somehow begun to reduce themselves, from the light and airy experiments he had started with, back to sinister collages of newsprint and then abstracts, of large, dark holes, assembled together, and finally to nothing at all.

But over the fireplace hung his last painting of the bay at Bealtra, with the marker point and the islands beyond, ablaze with fuchsia.

"That's really nice," said Siobhan.

"It's dreadful," said father. "Look at this, here." His finger stabbed at the paintwork, where it had exploded in a mass of violent brushstrokes across the canvas. "And here, and here again. Quite wrong. Romantic tosh. Picture postcard stuff."

"I think it's nice," she said. "Do you ever sell any?"

"Sell?" He started. "Sell! Of course not."

"You did. You did sell some paintings once," I said.

147

"Bah! Just to people we know," he said.

The sound of a brass band filled the street outside, playing "Silent Night."

"Hah! God-botherers!" cried my father, relieved at the interruption.

"Well now," said mother, coming through the door from the kitchen. "Anyone for a little light supper?"

Tom came in later, after the meal was over, flushed, with lipstick on his collar.

"Hi, guys," he said, helping himself to whisky and putting his feet up on the fender.

"Here! That's my whisky," said father, making a grab for the bottle, but Tom held onto it, waving it at him, just to wind the old fellow up some more, till he relented, and gave it back.

The only part of Christmas that father still seemed to enjoy was the lighting of the tree. Obediently we stood aside, as he fumbled for the matches, as if it were a particular kind of sacrament. We watched the candles burning down, silenced for a moment by their beauty, until the hot wax spilled over and the first branches began to smoke and smoulder, filling the house with the smell of pine. Still my father kept us from extinguishing the lights.

"There's more left in the candles," he said.

"Oh, put it out, Bernard, for God's sake," said my mother. "Put it out and let's all get to bed!"

But instead of going to bed, they started at it again. At first I'd thought we'd get through it, but we never did, even with the candles. Maybe the old man kept himself going a little longer than usual, and it was well past midnight, into Christmas Day when I was wakened by the sound of shouting, and Siobhan's voice shrill, telling them to not behave like eejits and to go to bed, and the other brother shouting out as to how the old fellow's ideas were bollocks, and himself shouting back that James should get some sense before someone taught him a lesson he'd not forget.

Then I heard the sound of the car starting up in the drive. I climbed out of bed, across the cold, moonlit bedroom, and looked down through the bare trees into the street below. There I watched my father reverse out down the drive, and, skidding in the road, drive away. The other brother came out in the road in shirtsleeves, still holding the champagne glass he'd toasted in the Christmas with. He was followed by Siobhan in her party frock. It had begun to snow, and the track marks of the car were quickly covered over.

At Christmas dinner the next day, there was a strange, empty atmosphere at the table.

"Well, I think that's done just right. I do the last half-hour over steam you know, with a sprig of rosemary," my mother poked at the turkey, knowledgeably.

"Yes, that's about done. What does everyone think?" We agreed it was done, and praised the stuffing, the cranberry sauce and the potatoes, even the sprouts.

"This is really excellent," echoed Siobhan.

"She's a dab hand at cooking alright." Afterwards, we retired to the sofa in front of the living room fire and watched "Mary Poppins" wordlessly. In the evening we asked where he had gone. My mother said she did not know.

"Look, we can have some of that breast we've set aside for him, with a little salad," she said, clearing his place away.

He returned the day after Boxing Day. The car was streaked in mud. We circled around him warily. The house had emptied, the presents were boxed.

"Where'd you go, Da?" I asked.

"Away," he said. "I went away."

His eyes avoided ours. "Over the border," he added. "To the sea."

CHAPTER FOURTEEN

After Christmas we went walking in the mountains, my brothers and I. The snow was hard packed under foot and the path curved round the side of the foothills, climbing away from the sea on our right. The Irish Sea that day was different to the west coast; it had a paler, less stormy complexion.

"So, Pats, what are you going to do?" asked Tom, our feet scrunching as we walked along with that hasty, competitive lurch we had all acquired. The wind funnelled through the gaps in the dry-stone walling as we passed, chilling us on an exposed cheek or bare forearm.

"I don't know."

"Are you going to England?" asked the other brother. "Mother wants you to."

"Get away, Pats," said Tom, as he vaulted over a gate, the path leading up ahead, climbing out up the side of the mountain, to the last stile that led out onto the moors beyond. "You've got to get away from here." We walked on, the wind at our backs now, climbing steadily, our breath freezing in the chill New Year air.

"You could go down to Dublin," said the other brother. "It's a fine place."

"I know." I'd spent a day there with Elaine, walking down by the Liffey.

When we breasted the first rise, the moor opened before us. Looking back, I could now see the patchwork geography of the map below; the intricate pattern of farms and cottages, tucked into the mountainside, decreasing in size the higher they got, until the weather had frozen or rained the crops out of the ground and rotted the hooves of the cattle as they grazed, and then the farming had stopped and the land went beyond human habitation.

The great bulk of the Mourne Wall lay in front of us, snaking away, our own Great Wall of China. We all laid our hands on it, to feel the smoothly quarried granite, the interlocking blocks, assembled there to keep all living things from the hills above. The stone felt icy to the touch as we clambered over. On the other side the whole range of hills opened to us, first Slieve Donard and Slieve Bignian, then the great jagged tooth of Bearnagh, names soon to be lost in the silent tread of the passing years in which the country one is born in slips into memory.

At the summit we stopped. The day was brilliantly clear. The other brother lit a cigarette and smoked it held upright, cupped behind his hand, slightly apart from us all. Tom stood looking down at the sea, impatient to be off. My eye followed the road, from Newcastle bay, across through the forest to the lakes and beyond to the village of Hilltown, with its two churches. Lost further out in the blue-green distance was the deep country of South Armagh. My eyes probed into the mist, trying to see that distant farmland and the white road, leading up the hill. But everything swam and merged before my gaze, and Ireland dissolved to the border: Cavan, Monagahan, Galway and, lost to view below the horizon, the Atlantic Ocean, raging and hammering against the rocks.

"C'mon, let's go," I said.

In the weeks which followed, Peter and I found some work to take our minds off things. Every afternoon we slipped from school and ran down the back alleys behind the city centre cinemas, and in through the stage door of the opera house. As we entered we heard the murmur of the audience through the faded curtains and saw the house lights were up for another matinée. Behind the scenes the stage was set out with a castle and Aladdin's cave and all the scenes to come, laid out and fixed in order ready for the show.

The dancers flitted to and fro, standing on their points, awaiting the overture. Nervously I stepped around them, behind the backdrop, where fantasy ended in a mess of brick-work and disused sets, and crossed in the gloom to the far side of the stage, saluting the stage manager where he sat at his high stool by the curtain, watching the clock with a Russian cigarette fuming in an ivory holder between his fingers.

I climbed the spiral stairs to the darkened fly loft where the fly gang were at their poker, the ebb and flow of their game marked by sighs and groans.

"Afternoon boys!" we said, in greeting.

"Patsy, Peter, my sons," they murmured in response. "C'mon and give us some of your money you wee cunts."

"Have you's got the castle done yet?" I asked.

"The castle's done. No thanks to you, ye skiving wee git," they said.

"C'mon and learn the rules o'the game, son."

"I'm for a smoke," I said, and joined Peter leaning over the balcony rail where the fly ropes were tied off, looking down at the stage below. I heard the orchestra starting up; a few saws and scrapes from the violins, a stray bump from the drum kit, the sound of the fat conductor clearing his throat, and then a short mournful tune to hush the audience and the voice of the stage manager down below snapping:

"Quiet please. Overture and beginners," in a stagy, English accent. The glow of Peter's cigarette illuminated his expression of supreme contentment, as he looked down on the dancing girls as they formed up, and then the stage lights went up and the curtain swept back.

"Jesus, would you look at the tits on that one," said Peter.

"Avert your eyes, Patrick my son."

"That'll make yez blind," came a low rumble of admonishment from the poker table. But I could not avert my gaze from the scene below. Everywhere seemed filled with dancing girls. The stage was hot and reeked of powder, elastic, faded red velvet curtains, Russian cigarettes and the faint, illicit tang of cannabis.

"So," at length the magician boomed, "So! Magic this castle away." Peter and I were hanging over the rail, watching the girls below, inhaling deeply, while behind us the poker absorbed the rest of the fly team.

"So! Magic this castle away!" shouted the magician below once more. I pulled on my joint, admiring the scene; the castle and its minarets, with the golden gate and the drawbridge, the magician in his thigh-length leather boots and ginger beard, the girls in fishnet stockings.

"Aha!" cried the magician desperately. "It seems my magic is not as powerful as once it was." The girls were quite beautiful, in every way. The stage lights glowed warmly. I would have a pint when the show was over. Then the stage manager's voice awoke me, drawling sardonically through the intercom.

"For God's sake fly gang, get that magic castle out of here!" We stumbled in the gloom and then began to haul, all of us, on the heavy ropes that'd get the magic castle out, up and away as the magician had commanded.

When spring came, my bedroom began to fill with paper, as the other brother's had before me. I'd done a schedule, which was taped to the wall, for my revision and used my father's example to claim privileges for the great work I'd promised them was in progress. Father's Mahler was silenced for once, and I was allowed to stay up late, far into the night, to study. But instead of studying I would watch the searchlights from the helicopters over the city, or play music softly on James's old gramophone.

One night, at about eleven the phone went, and my mother called me down. She had that pinched look about her again, and was holding the phone away from her like it smelt. At first

I thought it was because of the late hour, and the interruption to my studies.

"It's Elaine," she said. I took the phone from her.

"Hiya," I said, trying to sound cool. "How's things?"

"Not so bright," she said. "Me Da's been blown up."

Apparently, he'd been into Armagh to buy a new colour television. He'd just stopped the car outside the security gates, when a mortar bomb came in over the rooftops and went off in the main street outside the barracks. There was a few of them blown away on the day so he was lucky, she said. One of the wee bits of shrapnel had gone through his head, and the other one had nicked the base of his spine. They'd had him up at the Altnagelvin hospital, which Elaine said was one of the best hospitals in the world for this kind of thing now, and they were hopeful he'd improve. She thought she'd ring me to let me know, rather than to hear it secondhand.

"Are you okay?" I asked. "Shall I come down?" There was a bit of a pause at that. Under the circumstances, it wasn't the best time to come, she said.

I held the phone in my hand after she'd rung off. I wondered what circumstances she was referring to. There wasn't a lot to do. They were hopeful he'd improve. So there we all were then, I thought. Each in our corners. And wasn't it ironic that all along we'd been expecting something to happen to the other brother, who after all was in the thick of things, and it goes and happens to someone different altogether. That's what laughing at history got you. You might have expected something to happen to the other brother, but nothing much ever did.

CHAPTER FIFTEEN

I found the courage to drive down there on a showery April day just before my exams. The hedgerows along the way were full of blossom and the fields luminous with streaming water in the intermittent spring sunshine. The roads were empty and the country seemed more beautiful than ever, as if nothing had ever happened, as if miraculously, for one short moment, we had stepped back into some older, rural past that had never been. I smoked, with my elbow resting on the windowsill, the air almost unbelievably fresh, blowing in through the open car window.

As I came through the village all my old memories came back at me. I'd music on, to try and calm me, playing softly. I felt my stomach tighten, my skin tingled across my face. As I swung in by their house she ran out to see me, and leant in on the window, still in her slippers.

"How're ye doin?"

"Aye, alright. How's your Da?"

"C'mon in and we'll have some tea," she said, as if she had been expecting me all the time, though she seemed tense, nervous as if something that could not be prepared for were about to happen.

"You're looking thin," she said.

Inside the house was quiet, with just the clock ticking in the hall and the noise of a television set turned low murmuring from the parlour. She whispered as she made the tea, as if it were normal, as if that was what she would do now.

"We'd best be quiet while he's sleeping," she said.

With the tea done, she tapped on his door.

"Da?" she said. They'd propped him up in the living room, on the sofa in front of the big new television, with the best view of the window and of the fields falling away to the border beyond. His head did not move as we came in. The news was on the television; a fellow's car being lifted out by a crane, and the road taped off all around it.

"Da?" He'd put on a lot of weight and his skin had gone the sort of colour as if his blood no longer flowed so well. She walked round in front of him, so he could see her.

"You ready for tea, Da?" she asked. His head nodded very slightly, but he remained staring straight ahead.

"There's someone here," she said. He did not turn. Maybe he could not turn. He was still a big man; heavyset and strong across the chest. His eyes flicked sideways over me once, then back to the screen. Whether he had recognised me, I didn't know. She gave him his tea in a mug, on a saucer. The mug clattered on the saucer. She wiped at the carpet where the tea had spilt, with the cloth she'd brought with her.

"Get that wee fucker outa here," he said, clearly.

"Da," said Elaine. "Don't Da."

"I want that fucker out," he grunted, his hands gripping the sides of the sofa. She pushed me gently back towards the door. Outside on the step it was raining, a fine, soft spring drizzle.

"Come on, Elaine," I whispered.

"You'd best go," she said, her eyes desperate.

When I next went round to the other brother's place, it did not seem quite the same.

"Dear God would you look what the cat's brought in!" said Siobhan, and gave me a big hug, and I went in. The place smelt of gas, and it was dark even in summer.

"Hi, Pats," said James. He was smoking, with his shirtsleeves rolled up. The table was covered in papers and there were big boxes of papers against the walls too. He was scribbling away, and lighting himself another cigarette from the first.

"What're you all up to?" I asked.

"Oh, Sean's got him a job. You know Sean?" said Siobhan. "We worked together in Mid-Ulster. He's the boy. You've got to meet him."

Later in the evening, when it was dark, the flat began to fill up with fellows. The doorbell rang and a van delivered a couple of boxes filled with leaflets and posters of the army with the faces of pigs, and pictures of barbed wire and clenched fists. They asked me to help out, and to stuff some envelopes, but I made my excuses and left. Truth to tell, I couldn't reconcile any of it.

"And how's Elaine?" asked father. "We've not seen her for some time."

"How's her father? That was a terrible thing," said mother. "Terrible. And her so young. Her mother must be devastated."

I looked up. Father was tucking into his cereal with his spectacles on askew, his mouth working away from side to side as he chewed. The Irish Times was open on the table in front of him, with his pipe and tobacco and the ashtray already full of scrapings and match ends. Mother paused at the kitchen door, with her apron from the National Trust round her waist.

"You could ask her up," she said. "Just for a few days."

"I'm too busy. I've my exams." Like a sunken wreck, I thought. That was what it felt like now; a sunken wreck in your belly, with its spars all broken and smashed to bits, lying on the seafloor. Every time I thought about him, with his pale, washed out face and his swollen body and the scene with the television on, I felt the wreck there. Every time I thought about her I felt it too.

I could almost see it was on the tip of my mother's tongue to say, "Don't work. Take time off," but I could see the way she looked at father, as he aimlessly scoured out his pipe and lost himself once more in the farming reports, glancing up from time to time, almost surprised that we were still there.

"I think it's brightening up," he said, standing and stretching as he peered at the weather outside. "I think I might take a little stroll."

But then that evening there was a sudden, tremendous hammering on the front door and we went out into the hall, thinking perhaps there was a burglary going on, unheard of as these things were.

"What the hell . . . ?" began the old fellow, grabbing his umbrella from the stand in the hall, as the first thing that came to hand.

"Bernard!" shouted mother. And then the door came in and the hall was full of soldiers with their berets and body armour. Through the window I could see more running round the back, over the flowerbeds and in through the kitchen. Two of the men were away up the stairs and banging around in the attic and the cupboards up above before any of us could stop them. The officer stepped up. He was clean-shaven and slightly plump.

"James Grant?" he said to me. "Are you James Grant?"

"He's away. We don't know where," said mother.

"That bloody eejit," said father.

"I'm Patrick. Patrick Grant."

I recognised the epaulettes and the beret from the kitchen at Markethill, all those months before.

"We'll be a minute," said the officer, less belligerent when he heard my mother's accent. "We've to make sure." And then he was off up the stairs, two at a time.

My father seemed shocked at first, then strangely excited, as if someone had noticed him at last, and made him important, notorious even, as he had always wished to be.

"Well, well!" He said. "This is a turn up. A turn up indeed!"

At length the squad finished their search for James and came bounding down the stairs and back out into the street. The sentries they'd posted in the front flowerbeds next to mother's roses stepped back through the front hedge, and they all climbed into their armoured Land Rover and sped away, as quickly as they had come.

"Well!" said father again, while mother went round the house checking for damage.

"They could at least have closed the cupboard doors after them," she said. "And they' ve left a fearful mess in his room."

The neighbours came over.

"They wanted James," explained mother. "The army was up after James."

Now Cultra Avenue was a respectable Protestant street, and no one of course wanted these kind of events in such a place. As my mother explained, I could see all the neighbours tut-tutting and murmuring and drawing up conclusions. The neighbours indeed wrung their hands and said what a pity it was; hadn't James been such a lovely wee boy too, and now look what had become of him, wasn't it chronic? I could see them thinking if it wasn't for his mother being English and not understanding, and his father being a lecturer up at the university, well surely to God poor wee James would have grown up alright.

Peter came over to inspect the damage.

"So you hear they tried to lift James?" I said.

"Oh aye," he said. Not that the other brother was responsible for anything, these words being slippery to use. I didn't know what James was doing. I started to say this. I was babbling excuses to Peter, but he stopped me.

"What'd they want to lift him for?" he asked, knowing what for, as he well knew the other brother's views, as everyone did. But he was asking out of politeness, just the same, so I'd feel OK.

"You know how involved he's been," I said.

"How involved has he been?" he asked.

"Not much," I said. "At least not that I know of. You know. What's involved anyway?"

"We're all involved," he said.

We had a beer together in the Marlborough Inn, and strolled back through the park, buying a couple of cans along the way.

"How's Elaine?" I asked him, as we settled on a park bench by the ornamental pond and opened up our beers. "And how's her Da?"

"He's still the same," he said, and threw the can back and smacked his lips appreciatively. "Jesus Christ, this is good. How much is it?"

He counted the money in his pocket. "We'll have another of these, shall we?" he said, and then he told me about her father. When he'd finished, we sat in silence for a bit.

"Elaine's a different girl altogether," he said.

"Aye."

I was anxious to get away, but Peter had kicked off his shoes, enjoying the sun.

"Oh aye she's changed," he said. "I think she's gone crazy too. She should get out of there, you know. It's driving her nuts in that wee house with her Da laid up and everything that's going on. It'd do her good to get away. Oh aye. It'd be the very best thing."

Across the main road, down by the railway tracks, I could hear a drum starting up, the first heavy rolls of the Lambeg drums.

"Have ye decided where you're going?" he asked.

"I'm not going anywhere," I said. "I've finished with all that study. It never got any of us anywhere." I said it wildly, just to see what would happen. It felt like letting off a rocket, a blast bomb to me, as if I'd committed some great, relieving sin.

"Ach you shouldn't give up now," he said. "After all the work yez' ve put in." And now he sounded too old for his age. He was starting to bug me, he was so sensible underneath.

"You're so sensible, Peter. Here, give me some of that beer."

"I'm jest giving yez some advice that's all," he said. I knew he was right, that I should work. That I should not forget her. And that made me madder still with him.

The final lessons drew to a close at school.

"Was the Duke of Marlborough a statesman or a politician?" Our history teacher taught from behind a large map of the empire, which hung across the front of his desk. He had a handlebar moustache, which was yellow on the underside through his habit of smoking cigars behind the map.

"So, what was he . . . ?" The voice asked, as smoke drifted around the corners of the map, lapping India, and Ceylon, Australia. "A statesman, or . . . Grant! A politician?"

"A politician, sir. He had no long-term view. He pursued short-term gain and his own particular interest rather than the general interest."

"Good! Now McConochy, what examples can you give for Grant's hypothesis regarding the Duke of Marlborough, limited though it is?" The disembodied voice filled the room. The windows were open, the glass taped over against the blast from bombs. From outside came the noise of a mower on the cricket pitch.

"Malplaquet, sir. Sort of a short-term thing, wasn't it?"

"Perhaps," came the answer. "Perhaps it was and perhaps again it wasn't. Let us return to Grant's engaging, if limited hypothesis. Now McConochy. McConochy you are there, aren't you? . . .

And then almost too soon the examinations were over and we spilled out down the sunlit steps and ran, some throwing bags and books across the quadrangle as they went, out through the great wooden doors and away up the long drive and off into the city centre.

To celebrate, Peter and I set off up the coast the next day, along with Cyril and a girl he'd taken up with. We all met at

York Street at nine, and for me it was a bit of a relief to be just out for some fun. Cyril was larking around, doing accents and impersonations on the platform while the girl he was with looked on embarrassed.

"For God's sake Cyril," she kept saying. "There's people giving us looks."

Peter turned up ten minutes later, dressed in an old tweed jacket and heavy brown shoes.

"By Christ Peter, that's some rig out," said Cyril. "Is this your university gear or something?" Peter looked offended by this and showed us the leather elbow patches on the jacket he'd acquired, and explained how he'd got it for a bob in Smithfield Market.

"A bargain!" said Cyril.

But Peter was becoming distracted, and kept looking at his watch.

"She said she might come up, just for the crack," he said.

"Who?" I said.

"Elaine," he said.

"Why'd ye not tell me?"

"I thought ye'd be pleased," he said.

"I am. That's great," I said.

We bought the tickets.

"Shall we get one for her?" I asked. "Just in case?"

"Na," she'll miss it. "Always does," said Peter.

But then she came up, casually, not hurrying.

"Oh, hi you guys," she said, and kissed me and Peter on the cheek, in a sort of formal way I'd not seen before. She seemed a little thinner than when I'd last seen her. Older too, in some strange way that was hard to put a finger on.

"This is Cyril," said Peter.

Cyril bowed.

"And Anne. She's a friend of Cyril's."

"Anne McLaverty," she said. She'd a pale face, with papery skin. Just to look at her you could see she was an intellectual alright. Beside her, Elaine still looked amazing. But Cyril seemed not to notice at all.

"How's you all been. Still buried in them books?" she said.

We asked about her father, but now it was more of a polite thing as we knew there'd be no change.

On the promenade at Portrush everyone was out in their finery. The place was absolutely packed, like nothing I'd ever seen. We strolled along, with the distant waves lapping gently on the sands, and the beach crowded with families down below. Cyril had us all in stitches on the front reciting chunks out of Joyce he seemed to have learnt off by heart, in some sort of gobshite Dublin accent, while Elaine walked on a little ahead of us, slightly apart.

"It's a wee bit . . . eh, common," she said. I couldn't tell if she was joking, for her accent was part posh English, part Irish, like she'd put it on as an antidote to Cyril's performance.

"Ah, its grand," I said, "Absolutely cracking," in my thickest Belfast. By now we could do every accent from every corner of Ireland. It felt like we could be who we wished, for one day. Indeed it was a grand day, with the hot summer air and the light breeze and the bunting flying gaily. I held her hand, and she didn't seem to resist.

"So," Anne asked Elaine. "Were you's at Armagh Royal?"

"A long time ago!" she said.

And then suddenly they were all off again about which university they were going to. Cyril was away to Balliol. Peter was off to Trinity, Anne to Nottingham. At home I'd had the forms, but for weeks they'd lain uncompleted.

"Where're you's goin' ?" Anne asked me the question I'd not wanted.

"Keele," I said. It was all I could think to say. My parents had said it was a 'ghastly little place.' Then Elaine said suddenly:

"Why d'yez all have to go away?"

It was true, we agreed. Why did we all have to go away?

"Ah, but the die is cast," said Cyril, mock dramatic.

"It's too late now," said Peter gravely. "The decisions have been taken."

I wasn't sure they had, by me at least.

"Sure they'll all be back," I said.

"In the vacations," added Peter.

And then we had some beer outside a bar at the end of the promenade. The table was sticky with spilt drinks and popcorn.

"B' jez there's a fine heifer," said Peter, nodding across to a woman with huge, pasty thighs, who was squeezed into a pair of tight, mauve shorts.

"Imagine that one wrapped roun' yez," said Elaine.

We swam, and the sea was ice cold. It took the wind out of me, and shrivelled the erection that I'd had from watching Elaine strip, at least till she came up and started splashing me, her breasts bobbing, glistening in the cold seawater.

"Whew!" she cried, plunging herself under the water, and standing in the shallows, her costume clinging to her till I ducked her, feeling her wet body almost bare and slippery, struggling to escape.

"Why'd ye not ring?" I said to her close up, standing in the cold water.

She looked back at me, into my eyes.

"I couldna'," she said, as if to say, "What of it and what are you going to do about it." But I wasn't sure if it was part of the continuing game or what.

Back on the beach, she dried herself and tied her hair back, and rubbed on the suntan oil. I rolled over to face her, but her eyes were closed against me, lightly flecked with sand, though still fluttering so I knew she was not asleep. I tried to blot the others out, to create some intimacy.

"What're yez dreaming of?" I asked her quietly.

"Oh," she said, clenching her eyes tight as if trying to summon the images.

"Still dancing," she murmured.

"Dancing?"

"Oh yes," she said, in a low voice so the others couldn't hear. "I'm in a beautiful, beautiful ballroom on the edge of a lake. It is Vienna, or Switzerland. The tall windows open out onto the balcony, and the balcony leads down to a lake. Over the lake there are . . ." She paused. "Fireworks which light up a paddle steamer, one of them old ones, chugging across the water."

"And?"

"Shhh."

"Get on with it." I tickled her ribs and she squirmed.

"This handsome fellow comes up and asks me to dance, just as the band strikes up my favourite number." She opened her eyes. They were misty and far away, and suddenly I could see that she had not been thinking of me.

"Ah come on, that's hackneyed," interrupted Cyril loudly.

"Its what?"

"Hackneyed. Y'know, a cliche."

"Cliche?" she said, not understanding.

"What everyone dreams of," I said.

"There's nothing wrong with that is there?" She sat up crossly and rubbed on more oil. She reached for her clothes to make a pillow. As she bent down, I ran my hand down her back, leaving a trail in the moisture.

"Get off. That tickles," she said.

A silence fell, and I listened to the distant waves, the sounds of family conversations, of children at play, of cars on the road above the beach, and music from the open windows of the bars, and closed my eyes, the hot sun on my eyelids.

"D'ye hear me Da was nearly blown up," I said. There was no response from any of them, so I spoke more loudly. "Left his briefcase in the bar with the old alarm clock he uses to time the examinations."

"Ah, for God's sake," the others protested, disgusted with me for telling any kind of bomb story.

"And then when he went back the army had sealed the place off and brought in the sniffer robots.

"Robots can't sniff," objected Cyril.

"Alright, sniffer dogs then and a robot to blow it up. Blew the old fellow's briefcase to bits!" I paused. "Its true! Really! The old fellow was glad."

"Sure that's all bollocks," said Elaine. "His type's no chance of being hit."

"What d'ye mean by that?"

"The English," she said.

"We're not English." This was getting me cross now.

"Your Ma is. Its not the same for their type. They're lucky," she said decisively.

On one side of me, Cyril stirred.

"Stout!" he said.

On the other side of him, Peter smacked his lips, relieved at Cyril's interruption.

"Pint of double," he said.

"I'm for an ice cream," said Cyril's girlfriend. "Jeez it's too hot." Her skin was white, going red along the tops of her thighs. Cyril had kept his long trousers on all day.

"Cyril, will you not show us your legs?" said Elaine.

"My legs for Ireland's future," he announced, portentously.

"You're full of shit, Cyril," said Peter.

Along the beach the tide was far out by now, and it was beginning to cool a little. It was nearly time to go.

On the train home we were crammed in a compartment with some girls from Belfast on an outing, and Peter got out of control.

"Would you girls like to see my chest?" he asked.

"No, but I bet you'd like to see ours," they flirted back.

"I can see already, thank-you," he said, his tongue hanging out like a dog on a hot day.

But as the train started to go down the shore of Belfast Lough towards the city I could sense the anxiety burning in my stomach again. The windows were open and the mudflats dotted with seagulls. Soon the crane at Harland and Wolf came into view. Elaine got up and went out into the corridor. I went out too and intercepted her. The train bounced over the first set of points outside the terminus, throwing us together in the crush.

"Will yez not come with me?" I said.

"No," she said. "No, I can't," and she pushed past.

"Why not?"

"It's me Da," she said..

"Your Da?"

"He can't abide Micks," she said.

"We're not Micks. Not English, not Micks, not nothing," I almost shouted at her.

"I know," she said, holding my arm gently, "that's the problem," as the train braked sharply.

At the station, she hissed at Peter:

"Not a word, mind Peter," and touched her fingers to her lips.

Later that night we found ourselves half drunk outside a big church somewhere in the south of the city. Peter was there and Cyril and a couple of others from the school. We had smoked a little dope, and somehow caught by some passing spirit from the outside world, had picked some roses along the way. We slumped on a bench beneath the lych-gate, beset with painful laughter. Our hair was full of roses. Behind us the church was stern and dark and black, its steeple seeming to point accusingly at the sky.

"So," I said. "What do we do now?" A pair of lights came slowly up the deserted road. I tried to get up. Peter tried to get up. The lights stopped. They went on full beam, and dazzled us like rabbits. Then, out of the halo of light stepped four bulky figures, in bottle green uniforms and peak caps, wearing flak jackets.

"Evening, lads," said one. "Where did ye get them roses?"

CHAPTER SIXTEEN

All through the rest of that hot, endless summer I dithered on, through the marching season, while my father tinkered about and found excuses not to be away on holiday, or snapped and nagged at me to move on. I kept hoping that something would turn up.

"Can you not get a job or something?" said mother. "Here, look, we'll pay for you to get away," she added.

Cyril asked me down to their place in Ballymena for a weekend before he left, and gladly I went, just for the change of air. His parents were not to be seen, registering their presence only through phone calls every day or so, to see we were alright. Their house in the country was a solid, Edwardian affair, with a double garage. Cyril lay around in bed in the mornings reading the "Irish Times," "Fortnight" and the English weeklies too.

We took a couple of shotguns out shooting rabbits, for entertainment, walking along the country lanes till we saw them in the fields alongside, and then we were in through the hedgerows and blasting away until Cyril shot a hare, which put me off on account of the beast being so big.

"Ah, fuck me Cyril will you look at the size of it," I said. Stretched out with its limbs still twitching, it was nearly three feet long.

"There's a good bit of meat on him though," said Cyril, and insisted I hung it in his garage till it was time to get back to the city, but by then it was stiff and inflexible, and couldn't be fitted in a bag for me to take home. In the end we wrapped it in brown paper. Even then it was that long that its feet stuck out at either end, and I had to take the train back to Belfast with the hare under my arm.

On the way back from the station I visited Corporation Street, to sign on for unemployment.

"What' ye got in there, feller. Is it a dog or what?"

"A hare."

"Yez should keep them vertical son. They should be hung."

"Its been hung already."

"Yez could use it as a walking stick, eh?"

I gathered quite a bit of attention in the dole queue, so much so that the clerk at the counter took a dislike to me and gave me a job.

"Coming in here with dead animals under yer arm," he muttered. "Yez'd better git some work."

When I brought the hare home my mother was outraged.

"It'll stink the place out," she said. But my father hung it up with wire in the yard, and walked round it thoughtfully, poking it with his pipe.

"Fine set of whiskers on him," he said, sniffing appreciatively. "He's ripe for eating," he added, and skinned him up and cooked him, saying, "In the war these were worth a bob or two."

The job was not a pleasure; the fellow I was working with coughed and spat a bit to clear the taste of vomit from his mouth in the mornings. Then he sat on a pile of rubble and tried to do the laces on his boots. He wiped his forehead with a handkerchief, and then his hands on the front of his old muddy suit.

"The Jasus!" he said.

His trousers were hitched with a thick old leather belt. He spat on his hands and laid out his jacket carefully on some dry brickwork. Then he started at it with the pick.

"There you go. At 'em. Away to fuck!" he growled at the brick embankment, loosening the masonry out with his pick. "Away to fuck and at 'em the wee bastards!"

After a while with the pick he had a good pile of bricks at his feet. He wasn't sweating or out of breath. He pulled at the wall with short, angry movements, turning the pick from time to time. When the bricks began to get under his feet he said:

"Come on you," and watched as I tried to shovel them clear into the bin.

"Student?" he said. "Here, see this." He took my shovel, pulling me to one side and swept into the bricks with it as if they were feathers. When he finished, he undid the top button of his shirt. Underneath I could see a string vest, and his neck, brick-red and sprouting with grey hairs. I learned to follow his method and by lunchtime, we'd have taken a good bite out of the brick face. "That's a grand morning's work. A fucking grand bit of digging," he said. "C'mon and we'll away to tea."

At the end of the day he took his jacket up, shook the dust off it and slipped into it carefully, despite its lack of elbows and the patch of mud down the front.

"There you are now, Michael!" he said, talking to himself as he looked in an imaginary mirror. "That's the business," and we went to hand in our tools.

Down below in the cutting where we worked, hidden from the sunlight, with the traffic overhead, we were lost to the world. I didn't think of Elaine, except at night. In the day, I'd dig and fill the big iron tubs with bricks, then see the crane hoist them out and drop them back empty a minute later, to be filled again. In the evenings I'd go home and eat big meals, before falling asleep in front of the game shows on the television.

The hole I was digging got gradually deeper. I began to find it hard to get up in the mornings. I was tortured with memories, going far back, so faint I was not certain if they were dreams or not.

Elaine wrote me a long letter in a huge, swirling hand that covered page after page in flowing prose:

I've been listening to music again. Sometimes when I lie on my bed and watch the country outside, I can see what these things mean. The clouds today are very pale, like distant dreams. Sometimes, you can see faces in the clouds, and sometimes there is nothing in them. This morning the rain came in from Cavan. You can see it, slanting before it falls. You wonder whether it'll fall here. I watched it come up over the road, bending in the wind, and then it came against the windows, with a first few drops, and then it clatters down, steaming on the paths, and the view's gone completely. Do you know they shot the postmaster in Markethill? I expect you's have the same where you are. Write to me.

"Did you never think about getting hitched, Michael?" I asked him one day. He stopped digging, and wiped his brow.

"Indeed I did not," he said, and spat in the bricks. "I wouldn't say no to a good wet hole now and again though boy. Oh no." And then he was at the bricks again.

"Jesus, no," he said, between clenched teeth. "A wee filly. That'd be just the ticket. There, Patsy, you can clear that lot away." The job was nearly done now. We'd gone down twenty feet, and the shuttering carpenters and scaffolders were coming up behind us, shoring the earth with steel behind us, before the concrete was poured in. The work slowed, and Michael began to get restless.

"There's no more than a week in it," he said. Then we were all out on our ears, back on the street.

Desperately, I rang for Peter and Cyril on the off-chance that they might be home, but there was no reply. That night I wrote her a note:

Dear Elaine,

I have decided to leave Ireland for good. I don't know if this is the right decision to take, but I can see no future here. I've booked a ticket for the 30th October on the Heysham boat. If you are able to come, please meet me in the bar in the second class. Otherwise the place will drag you down and suck you in, and I love you too much to see that happen. I do not know if we will get on or not, but we all stand a better chance elsewhere.

CHAPTER SEVENTEEN

I found mother with the Daily Telegraph open on the property pages one morning. There were adverts for cottages drenched in flowers: in Torquay and Paignton, the Lake District and the Cotswolds.

"Do you never think of moving?" I asked her.

She stopped for a moment, half guilty, then put her face together.

"Oh no," she said. "We could never afford to. What would I do over there? I've got all my friends here." She paused. For a moment, she sounded like Peter's grandmother, snapping at the cats. Then I realised she was lying to me about not wanting to go, and I couldn't see why.

"It's Bernard. He'll not go now," she said.

Later she came up to my room and started to clear the drawers. She had several sheets of new lining paper over one arm, and a big laundry basket in the other, and into it she began to put my clothes. We stripped the bed. I went to the window and sat on the old trunk, looking out over the plane trees. Outside, the leaves were beginning to curl and go brown and the twisted branches were becoming visible below. Between my teeth, for the last time, I felt the thin whistle of that song, starting up as it had when I was a child:

> *Then, hey, hey, ho, the lily, lily oh*
> *The loyal, royal, lily oh!*

Over the city the green hills looked down, the very same as they had been on the first day my mother came, and had been so thrilled by them.

My father took me to his study. Everything was covered in a

layer of dust. The window was closed tight against the air, the table strewn with bills. He searched amongst them, to show me what he'd been working on, holding the picture carefully against the light, squinting at it.

"Look, see this," he said. The picture was in an old gilt frame, and the gilt had peeled off. It was one of those part oil, part tapestry creations that you can get in the junk shops for a bob or two, and he had been restoring it. Across a river there strode the bold King William, to do battle with the Papists. Half of King William's shoulder had been eaten by moths, but my father had carefully tried to restore it with gold thread, and painted in the section of mountain where the paint had flaked off the canvas. The brushwork was a little unsteady.

"It's a brilliant bit of fudging," I said.

He looked at me, and for a moment, there was a bit of the old sparkle.

"Hah!" he said, and smiled a wee secret smile.

He took me for a drink in the Crown. We sat on the red leather seats, a little awkwardly, as he had limited his duties in every way imaginable, and when the time came to undertake them, he had lost the habit. His eyes were a little watery now, and his hand shook. He seemed on the point of saying something specific.

"We've time for another," he said instead. Overhead, the gilded mirrors reflected back the Victorian splendour of the bar: the marble columns, the polished brass, the staff in their black waistcoats.

"Very good, Mr Grant. I'll be right with you, sir."

Then when the drink had come, and he'd wiped at a bit of the spill with a beer mat, and jiggled his foot up and down as he did when there was something troubling him, he talked about how I should study hard, and how important it was to take the right decisions, and not to throw things away. I nodded numbly.

"Oh God," he said, draining his glass. "I'd better go." I got up too, but he gestured at my drink, barely touched.

"No. Finish your drink," he said.

Curious as to the reasons for his uncharacteristic abstinence, I followed him to the door, and watched him as he walked away, slightly unsteady on his feet, a little stooped, still wearing his old felt hat.

At the end of the street a woman crossed the road towards him, pushing a pram. My father chivalrously stepped forward and helped her lift the pram over the curb. The movement was strangely intimate, and too familiar, as his hand touched her back and he leant his head close to her's, solicitously. Together they walked round into Great Victoria Street, towards the cab rank. I followed at a distance. Once, he swung his walking stick around on his wrist, like Charlie Chaplin. The baby was crying.

"Oh God," I heard his voice carried by the wind. "That boy again."

I followed them up to the station, past the now burned-out hulk of the opera house, its blackened windows hosting pigeons, the frames blown out and shuttered with corrugated iron. Outside the Europa Hotel I could see him folding the pram while she held the child, still squealing.

The driver tried to help him, and I could see him talking back. Though I was too far away by now, I could imagine the words:

"No, no, let me do it. There's a little catch I've made. Just here."

As I turned to go, their taxi swept past me, my father's face a blur at the window. It was beginning to rain now, a heavy thunderstorm. I found myself standing outside the Presbyterian headquarters, all grim black stone and gargoyles. From there I could look right up the Grosvenor Road to the Falls beyond, and the mountains, rising up, a faded green in the gathering dusk. It was a warm evening, with a soft, damp wind off the sea. I felt very alone. He had almost bowed, and shuffled awkwardly as we had parted, strangely shrunken. Or perhaps it was I who had grown.

I pushed my way back through the swing doors into the Crown, and sat down on the red leatherette seats, with a pint of Guinness. The television was playing, ignored, high up against the far wall. It was a quiet time of night, before the crowds came in. The barman lingered over the froth, skimming it off in a leisurely way.

"Pint of double, coming up," he said.

So I had another pint, and then another, and when I came out it was completely dark.

"Why'd you marry him?" I asked mother, before I left.

"He was always handsome," she said.

"And at Oxford he was brilliant." I thought of the photographs of him there that we had in our album; in shirtsleeves with cool, cotton trousers and horn-rimmed spectacles, a mass of black hair over an intense, serious face with the eyes dark.

"It was almost unnatural. It was like a dividing line between genius and madness, divided but never resolved. Through his entire life, he could have gone either way. Well," she said, turning to her tea and newspaper again, "that's that."

The pier was crowded with soldiers, laughing and smoking, their kit bundled beside them, their vehicles lined up to descend the ramp into the hold, engines screaming, disturbing the gulls and drowning out our goodbyes.

When I too leaned on the rail, looking down at my mother and father, they were standing a foot apart, father with his pipe fuming away, looking at his watch and fidgeting, and mother with her hands held tight together, very upright, looking up. In the background I could hear the jukebox playing, "A whiter shade of pale," and the troops cheering as the lines

176

were cast off, and the oily water seeped in between boat and quay.

Down on the quayside, my mother and father waved. The water at the stern boiled, and the ship began to drift from the quay. Here and there people shouted back to those on shore, or made gay jokes while the ship seemed to hang there in the stream. But then, with a final blast on the siren, the engines raced, and we fell quiet.

I saw them turn away, my father's hand tentatively on my mother's shoulder, as we swept slowly out down the river, past the prison ship and the shipyard, leaving the Albert Clock behind, leaning slightly on one side in the sunset. Then we gathered speed away out across the estuary, until all that was left of Ireland was a purple smudge on the horizon with a band of evening sunlight blazing on the water around it.

I went down to the bar. It had a low ceiling and was fitted out in green plush. It was packed with soldiers and so thickly smoky it hurt your eyes. I scanned the bar carefully, from end to end. But she was not there. She had not come.

POSTSCRIPT

One memory sometimes comes to me, whenever I am in heavy London traffic or perhaps delayed on a crowded train at some suburban junction: I'm standing on the strand at Bealtra with the fisherman, who's got a big rusty scythe in his hand. Under my feet the hard white sand is covered with a thin sheen of clear, fresh water from the mountain river that empties in the bay. The noise of the Atlantic Ocean can be heard; the dull, booming whistle and suck of the surf beyond the dunes.

"Here's how you do it," says the fisherman. He was a young man, with a handsome, sunburnt face and heavy black hair, his arms strong.

"Gi'us the' bucket," he said, smiling at me. "Are yez ready?"

I nodded that I was and he leant over towards the sand, as if preparing to scythe away thistles, or nettles, and drove the old blunt blade downwards with a sudden angry movement.

I looked down at the water running through my six year old's sandals, cooling my toes, now no longer clear but muddied with sand as it tickled my feet, wondering what my mother would say and thinking how my father would find it interesting. And then he drew the blade through the sand suddenly, cutting it with wide angry swipes and semicircles as silver snakes burst everywhere around our feet, the fisherman laughing and scooping them into the bucket with his big hands. I screamed at first, then did what I could to help him put the eels in the bucket.

"From Belfast?" he asked afterwards.

"Aye," I said.

He nodded, a hint pityingly, as if that explained everything about me.

"Have yez ever been there?" I asked.

"Ach no," he said, as if the idea were ridiculous, almost as funny as my attempts to catch the eels as they burst from the sand at my feet.

My other recurrent memory which sometimes comes as I lie in bed, mulling things over, is this: I am out shopping, although I cannot remember for what precisely. The absence of a list, or purpose is overwhelming me; I feel my mind working leadenly, sluggishly. Was I meant to be getting shoes at Curtice's? What was it that my mother wanted me to buy? And I feel foolish about returning without the item I was asked to get. Ah, it is photographs for my bus pass! I place the money in the slot of the photo booth. It is ten forty-eight precisely (the memory seems cluttered with such details). I smile at the camera in the booth, which is whirring and clicking. I've the orange curtains pulled over, and there's a crowd of lads outside slicking back their hair with Brylcreem, waiting to take my place. The camera flashes, once, twice, three times and I pull a face for the fourth, squinting and turning up the corners of my mouth. As I do so, there's a huge blast in the street outside and when I come out the station is full of dust and people running.

I take refuge in the Washington Bar, watching the news. They say there's been a blitz in Belfast.

"D'ye hear Oxford Street's gone?" they say at the bar. The barman, gravely impassive, wipes the glasses with the white linen dishcloth, expressionless, as you do. Maybe though if you look closely, and perhaps I imagine this, there's a slight, perverse hint of satisfaction in his expression. The blast has made him not merely a barman, but a Belfast barman. Later he will be not merely a Belfast barman, but the barman at the Washington Bar on that particular day.

"Double," he says, scooping the froth from my beer. I've the photos still sticky in my pocket, and take them out to look.

The fourth photo has my eyes suddenly frightened, looking out to the side, to the curtains, trying to see where the blast has come from.

"That's grand," I say, taking the beer and giving him the money. "That's just what I need."

Still he says nothing, but strolls back to the till, and tosses the money in. The television is issuing warnings now. The barman and the old reprobates look up, mildly interested, as you would watching the odds for the horses. There's warnings for the Washington Bar, and the Dock Bar. Even then their movements are a bit slow. The barman hangs up his dishcloth, closes the till and locks it with a key attached with a chain to his belt. A couple of the reprobates fold their papers carefully, grumbling that it's a fucking liberty and a shame to have to move when they've a whole pint to drink. I take a good big gulp of my beer and step outside. It's a fresh autumn day. The street outside is completely empty except for a fellow on a bicycle, who's got past the roadblock where they've sealed the street, and in the middle of the road there's a car pulled over with both doors open. The only other fellow in the street is about a hundred yards away, a soldier crouching in a doorway .

"C'mon," says the barman and drags us back in through the bar, and out the back way past the empty barrels, with the kitchen ventilator blowing out the smells of chips and greens, cooking up for lunch. We half walk, half run, down an alley and round the corner into a normal street full of shoppers and the bomb goes off with a dull crump, and a few bits of light, dusty debris fall on us, like rain from the heavens.

A woman walking with a child in front of me screams, and clutches her forehead. Her child stops, curious, and looks up, but her mother is okay. There's a tiny trail of blood, where a fragment of glass has cut her face.

And then finally my memory is of them on the quayside that

evening. And of her with her hand trailing in the water as our dinghy drifted down the estuary, laughing at history. She was just eighteen, and completely alive.

London August 2000